No Romance

Without FINANCE

PART 1

Ricky Harper

I dedicate this book to all the women who know their worth. Your support and presence empower us (men) to thrive. I hope you receive the message without fixating on the title. I want to clarify that this book was written in a free flow as if you and I were sitting on the front porch talking to one another, without following any specific chapters as it flowed directly from my mind is how I wrote it. I aim to introduce a new approach to writing in all my books. The first step was to believe in myself and here is proof that I took a major leap of faith in a new direction, I promise to remember where I come from, and I appreciate my past as I embrace my next. Cheers to all the New Authors out here and those who aspire to become one.

Ricky Harper

"What's up girl?" "Girl nothing much. I'm just ramping up for Biker Week in South Carolina." "Myrtle Beach! Here we come, "says Shante doing a twerk dance. Shante, Jerria, Linda, Rita, Eve, and Kim all met in college. They attended Austin Peay together and graduated years ago. They got their education and fiercely took on the world. While Shante was dancing, Kim was edging her on saying, "Aye aye aye aye, "while smiling. Both girls are social workers for the state of Tennessee. Rita, Eve, and Kim were now licensed practical nurses and Linda is a real estate agent with a bachelor's degree in finance. They're all from Chattanooga Tennessee and after graduation they moved back home to begin their jobs. All six girls had dated guys throughout college that didn't work out and left them feeling as if relationships are a waste of time. They had met at Pier 88 restaurant in Chattanooga to have ladies chatter about life. They meet up every second Sunday to relax and take a break mentally from their careers. It's just May, and it has been a steady 5 months into the year for the women. They are all independent and they let the world know every chance they get. Shante, Jerria, and Kim live together in a 4-bedroom house in East Brainerd. Linda lives in Hixson in a 4-bedroom house. Rita and Eve live in the Highland Park area right up the street from each other in 4-bedroom houses also. On that note, each of them believes love can wait because the bills will not wait. All six women were there having drinks and venting. "That big ass booty. What man in their right mind wouldn't want to wake up to that," says Rita about Shante? Shante stops dancing, smacks her lips and twitch her hips from side to side while tilting her head and looks over at Rita and says, "Well the problem is that every man wants to wake up beside me, but I'm asking who wants to take care of me? What man ready to compensate me for all the pleasures I give? I'm 29 years old. A college graduate making over $50,000 a year after taxes. NO kids and no health or mental issues. Explain to me why I haven't found anybody? Shid, I know my pussy good, so explain," Shante says while taking a playful pouting slouching seat. Kim looks at her and takes a double shot of Casa Migos and says, "Girl look at all us sitting here. All of us are a catch. Kim, I feel ya girl. I feel the selection on men is just too got dam low. When we graduated there were 470 students that walked across the stage at

Austin Peay. Only 120 were men. Out of that 120 there is no telling what percentage is gay nor there is no telling how many of those men still believe in black love. You know the world paint the picture of dividing us and it's kind of quite sad the world has succeeded in doing so. How I would so much love a black king that's taller than me. Not a street guy, but an edge to him. And no! I am not settling," Kim says in a sassy playful voice. Eve lets out a big sigh and playfully slouches in her seat. "Bitch what's all that for, "says Kim to Eve playfully. Eve looks up at her and grab her shot glass off the table and says, "Well when you hoes stop complaining and accept these niggas for what they are, then your lives will be a little bit stress free." All the girls playfully taunt her to put them up on game then. "Well, it's quite very simple in my eyes. They are just another form of an ATM machine in my eyes. If no money is coming from them then I have no use for them." Jerria sips her long island iced tea and says, "I ain't saying she a gold digger." All the girls playfully finish the line and loudly cheer, "But we ain't messing with no broke niggas. They all laugh and give each other high fives and Linda chimes in and says, "Eve, I don't blame you............. Y'all know what, Fuck these niggas. I say we make a pact with each other." Jerria interrupts her after noticing how slow her words are and says, "Girl how many shots have you had." "This my eighth one and I am grown so that does not matter. And drunk or not, these men of today are not living up to the standard of being my man. Shid I can do bad by myself. Or if I wanted to constantly tell you to do something I will just have a child". "And even with that, you can't get away from the no-good motherfuckers cause u need a dick to make that happen naturally," Linda says as all of them bust out laughing. She continued, "For real though. Let us take another shot at a pact right here. Right now. That we are saying fuck these niggas and we gone look at them how our homegirl Eve said we need to look at them. ATM machines. Right bitch," she says twisting her neck and snapping her fingers. Eve looks at her and gives her the same energy back. Linda continues, "If they not coming off no bread, then they can't lay in my bed. I think I want to be a hoe this summer." They all started laughing and clung their shot glasses together and took a shot to the head. Eve reached over and told Linda, "Girl give me your glass. That's enough for your drunk ass. Just eat your food so you can have something on your stomach." Time goes by in the night as they continue enjoying each other's company with one another. The whole night the women were sizing men up. Recreationally flirting, but not going to far with the tease. Each woman paid for their own tab at the restaurant and gets up to leave. Each woman in the group are definite head turners. As they were gathering, they things they demanded the attention of every male eye there and a couple of women also. The waitress for the table they were sitting at had been eyeing Kim the entire time. Nice looking young lady. 5'9, 176lbs, dark brown eyes, Great teeth with full lips that attracts the masses. Breast that says look at me with naturally long hair that comes to her collar bone. Pure brown skin with a glow as if she stays hydrated from water. Kim leaves her a twenty-dollar tip. The waitress smiled at Kim and asked her, "Is there anything else you would like tonight, "she seductively says while taking a step back to give her a view of all of her. Black pencil skirt and a white button-down blouse with cleavage showing. Flirty but not slutty. Heels, NO lashes, foundation but not caked on makeup, and MAC lip gloss to highlight her lips. You can tell she was raised by an older woman with class. Kim caught the flirtatious savvy in her voice and replied, "Nah, not at this moment boo. But um, If I ever do need anything. You will find out, "Kim says with direct eye contact and the waitress smiles and says, "Well do not ever hesitate to try other things on the menu that's not in your comfort zone. You might make it your main dish." The waitress puts her twenty-dollar bill in her cleavage slowly as each of the girls were impressed with her choice of words. As they are walking out Eve says, "Looks like every lesbian we run across be trying to turn you out girl." "Welp it's flattering, but this pussy is strictly dickly baby. If it wasn't naturally born with a dick, then don't send it my way. Nothing against anyone else's preference but I have my own preference of what arouses me." "At this point, if that bitch got enough coins, I might let her eat this pussy. But I'm not touching that bitch, "Rita says in a drunken voice. Each girl burst out laughing calling her delusional and telling her she is curious and that the act alone is gay.

    Kim and Jerria went straight home. They both had shower on their mind, but Jerria got there first. She sat her lotions out for afterwards with her night garments. She put just as much into going to sleep as she did into going out. She undressed and put her cream silk robe on from Victoria Secret. Her hair came down to her perky breast. Perks from her father being from Saudi Arabia. Kim was walking up the stairs and caught a glimpse of Jerria and said, "Dam girl. Fuck that waitress. If I ever want some pussy, I will just try my bestie. With your sexy ass." "Don't start that gay shit girl. My pussy throbbing right now to. I might just climb that tree right about now," Jerria says with a jokingly smile. "Girl get your little ass in the shower. And don't come downstairs rubbing on yourself and shit. Put your lil lotions on up there in the room. I told you I'm strictly dickly but don't become my little secret tonight."

"Bitch let me find out I got your mind curious," Jerria laughs and shut the door. She looks in the pantry and grab her dildoe that mounts on the wall. Put her phone on the bathroom Bluetooth and prepare her walls to be penetrated by her lil fun toy. She slowly washed her body to the lyrics of Chris Brown as that's the pandora station she chosen. Once she was clean, she turned the shower head towards her toy so that the water could hit the toy and her pussy at the same time. She turned sideways and put her left hand on the shower door as her right hand reached back and guided her toy into her walls. "SSSSSSS," she says as the dildoe spreaded her pussy lips. She slides back slowly letting her womb take on the toy. Once she get her insides used to girth, she slowly starts slamming her pussy on the wall repeatedly. Lifting her breast up licking her own nipple while fucking herself. Repeatedly throwing that ass back, she begins to rub her clit side to side at the same time talking to the dildoe as if it was a person. "Mama pussy feel good to ya. You should feel special to sample this," she says in a moaning voice. Starting to feel her insides warm up and get pussy getting more wetter from sensation that she is giving herself, she says, "Hmmmm there it go. OOOOOOO fuck." She jerked as her pussy came and her eyes started rolling to the back of her head as she loudly moaned with excitement of releases the long night down her leg into the tub. After she was done, she came off it and turned around to clean it and kept talking to it. Stroking it with her hand and soap she says, "You the only dick that's gone get to experience me with no money involved. Dam...... That sounds like a prostitute a lil bit," she looked up at the ceiling whispering to herself. Humped her shoulders up and quickly said, "O well". Kim was downstairs on the phone with her brother Brandon. He was flying in town for the summer. He plays professional basketball for the Portland Trailblazers, and they were just eliminated from the playoffs. Brandon 6'10, dark skin, with light facial hair. Nappy hair, but he keeps it groomed. 260lbs with pearly white teeth. "Lil sis you still got that extra room I can use while I'm home right". "Yea it's still empty. Long as you don't mind waking up to Shante and Jerria worse' em ass." "Hell, nah I don't mind. Imma be there for three or four months, so don't get mad if I end up fucking one of them. Shid maybe both but forget that. Did you ask the owner what they wanted for the house? I just bought a house out here. I might as well have one at the crib for you." "Yea. The guy told me he wants $385,000." "Okay. Tomorrow, I want you to call him and tell him you have a full offer with cash, but he must pay the closing cost. Also, we got to start some businesses lil sis. I'm not going to be playing basketball to much longer." "Okay. Well, I will see you tomorrow and have an answer from the owner by the time you get here. Love you." "Love you too." They hang up and Kim looks at the time to see if its 9pm so she could take her birth control pill. "That's why that ass done got phat and spreading. That pill and that lil fake ass dick up there", Kim says jokingly. "Bitch fuck you. Its less headache than these niggas we were just talking bout." "My brother on his way in town. They done lost and he basically on break til training camp." "Girl then fuck me climbing yo dried up ass tree. I might have to climb that mountain of a man. Plus, he single with millions to blow. O yea. I gots to give him some pussy." "Well, he plans on spreading his man hood to all y'all. Just like every other man would be thinking. Ion know what these niggas see in y'all hoes," Kim playfully says with a playful stank face eating some lays potato chips. "Shid I'm not tripping on his pimping. As long as he spreads the wealth to this bitch, ion to much care and them hoes bet not either cause he not neither one of our nigga." "Now I'm not bout to let y'all just turn my brother to know trick." "O but your brother can turn your homegirls into hoes," Jerria says with a bitch please playful face and continues, "Nah bitch. We gone use these niggas as atm machines and your brother is no exception. We find another rich nigga and include you. You just can't get in on this one because he your brothers." They laugh out loud. Shante walks in at the end of their conversation. Kim lets Shante know that Brandon will be there tomorrow for 3 4 months. Shante gives Kim a sexual sneaky look and puts an extra twitch in her walk. Jerria catches it and says, "Girl she already talking about he off limits even though he says he trying to get at all of us. He fair game if he is breaking bread right," Jerria looks at Shante trying to get reassurance from her home girl of no jealous competition. "Big Bruh gone be just fine Kim. And Jerria he not my nigga or yours so you right. Break em girl," Shante playfully says seductively. The three women discuss going to Myrtle Beach for Biker weekend and more things they got planned for the rest of the year.

"Can I get a coffee with crème and sugar. I will also take two sausage and egg McMuffins please". "Drive around for your total please," the McDonald drive through host says. Eve headed to work. She works at Erlanger Hospital on 3rd Street. "That will be $11.87" Eve hands her a bank card. She swipes the card and gives her the receipt to sign. "Thank you. Here's your food and coffee. Condiments are in the bag. Have a great day". "You do the same baby. Thank you, sweetheart,", Eve says to the young lady. She pulls off and turns her music up as she eases her way back into morning traffic. Eve shift starts at 7am and she eating the McMuffins like she hasn't ate in years. She gets to the building early everyday just to catch up on girl gossip.

It's 6:30 when she gets to the break room at work. "Bitch you could have called and seen if I wanted something," says Rita in a playful voice. "And this my second one also girl. It's hot too girl. This is my second one, so if you want a piece then here you go," she says extending the McMuffin towards her as an offering. "Nah I am just kidding girl. I bought some shit off the lil food truck that comes every morning. I am soooooo ready to get this day over and done with girl, but that lil pharmaceutical rep that comes through here, I am going to have to put my fangs in him." "I know you are not talking about the white man that look every bit of 50. Girl, he married." "Please tell me what that got to do with me." "Shid, I guess nothing, but you know white people kinky." Rita looked at Eve with a smirk and says, "I am counting on it." Eve laughs and tells her, "Girl go clock us in before they fire me and yo freaky ass." They get their day started while Jerria was up at home getting ready for work. She clocks in at eight in the morning along with Shante. Sometimes they carpool together, but not today. Jerria looked at her phone and seen a text from Junior. His name is Ricky, but he is a Jr, so he goes by that. He texted her saying, "Good Morning." She smiled and called. "Awwww you up thinking about me. Let me find you got a thing for lil Jerria." Ricky Jr also is in the NBA. He plays for the Orlando Magic, but he is Brandon and Kim's cousin. He is 6'4 226lbs solid athletic lean muscle. Twenty-four, light skin dread head. Just signed a deal with a new shoe company for ten million. He is also home for the time being. "Yea we are still on." "Before I hang up though. What do you make a hour?" "I know you not asking for money." Ricky Jr did not even respond. He just burst out laughing. "21.50" "You get eight hours, right?" "Right." Ricky started mumbling figuring numbers to himself. "What are you saying under your breath over there?" "Hold on, I am calculating." "Boy!" He cut her off and said, "First off, I am not no boy. Today you're going to make $172 dollars. Right. If you call in right now and come, take some dick this morning. I will give you a week's pay for today, but you're my slave for today." A big smile went across her face and said, "Send me the address." "Bet." They hung up. She called her supervisor immediately and made up a lie on the fly. She had her personal number. "Good morning Mrs., Whitlock." "Child why are you calling me on my personal number. You must want something." "It's not that I want something, but a family emergency just came up. I need today off. I found out some disturbing news." Jerria voice was Oscar worthy. Angela Bassett would have been proud of the performance she was putting on. "Okay Jerria. I hope everything is fine. Deal with your family and get back here in the morning. Even though I know your lazy ass lying. You should have just called and asked for today off and said you will make it up on one of your off days. Now you putting karma on one of your family members to possibly have something bad happen to them, but you take the day. Lying heffa." They both laugh it off and get off the phone. Jerria looks at the text she has received from Ricky Jr and it's the W Hotel downtown Chattanooga with the suite number he is in. She cleans herself up and heads over to him. Her eyes was sparkling and a pulsating feeling was around her pussy from the view she was receiving because he answered the door naked. "So, you just standing there and let someone walk by and see me naked?" She walked in with butterflies in her stomach as he gently took her hand and guided her slowly pass him to enter the room. He let the door close behind her and latched the door. Immediately he demanded in confident voice, "Take your clothes off. But look at me while you doing it. And not like a kid going to bed. Take them off as you are trying to seduce me." He sat his phone to the Bluetooth he has set up in the room to give her a rhythm. Reggae came through the speakers. She kind of smiled at him in hesitation and he said, "Remember you agreed to be my slave." "I see you were for real demanding a bitch out of her clothes upon arrival." He swiftly grabbed her firmly by her throat and made her look up to him to let her know he means business, but she is not in danger. She moaned and dimmed her eyes. He didn't even have to say anything. While looking up at him she unbuckled her pants and started moving to the rhythm of the music. He let her go and watched her tease. She turned around after her pants were off and took her shirt off slowly. She through it back over shoulders and slowly took her bra off and let it fall to the floor. Turning around with her right arm holding her breast and her left hand made its way to her clit as she swirled it while grinding to the rhythm of the music. She walks over to him and whisper, "JerriaGetit with a dollar sign at the beginning." He smiled and said, "Women and money." "Niggas and their want for pussy. When my phone ding from the notification of receive, you will get everything you want. That's when I become your slave right," she says in a sexy flirtatious way while now rubbing her body against his. He backs from her and grabs his phone and transfers the money. She hears the notification and goes straight into submission mode which turned Ricky Jr on even more. He took her to the 8ft by 8ft walk in shower and let her wash him up and he washed her up. Lifting her in the shower, he pinned her against the wall and passionately kissed her neck. She moaned and just held on for the ride as she anticipated dick to enter her. He gave her passionate sex in the shower, washed themselves off and went to the room to give her aggressive sex. He had her in exhaustion as she just laid naked in the bed on her stomach and says, "Dam boy. Either you making sure you get your money worth, or you just been crushing on me. Which One is it?" "Well, you will be surprised at the energy the body gives you when you don't drink sodas nor have a big sugar intake. Shout out to what I put in my body when it comes to my stamina. Now to answer your question, I definitely was going to get my money worth, but your fine ass is definitely a crush of mine." "Why you have never said anything?" "Because I know way to much about you and to be quite honest…………Jerria ain't none of y'all shit, but you and your homegirls sexy ass hell." "Oh you can fuck on me, but not be with me." "Man, Jerria I literally tried to talk to you before I went pro and turned me down in college. I get to the league and now u willing to fuck me but even what we just did was good, but I had to pay for it." He laughed. "Well baby you offered. I probably wanted to fuck you anyway. And for the record, my mama and aunties told me No Romance without Finance." "And what does that even mean." She put her hand on her hip as she got out of bed naked and said, "It means that I bet not get a wet ass for nothing." "So, if we both understand that, why you trying to switch up with an attitude like I am tripping for offering to pay for it." She got quiet. "Exactly," he said while chuckling. He quickly just headed to the shower, and she joined him. "I was wondered what women put in they spend the night bag," he says jokingly laughing while looking at her remove things from her bag. She looks up and playfully smirks. They both put on some clothes, and she ask, "So since I am your slave for today, where we going today massa," she says the last part in jokingly slavery voice and quickly sets her straight. "Look as long we ever around each other, we not gone ever disrespect the people that went through that shit with any mockery. I know massa and I know you was just playing, but that's not funny and shouldn't be to any person of color." "Dam I was just playing baby. Why so serious?" "Shid I will ask why we as a people not serious enough about that topic? Imma change the subject though because that's gone go way too deep. And this is not the day for that, but you can stay here or ride with me to pick my cousin up from the airport. Shid, I got to take him to y'all house anyway, so if you wanted to chill back at your crib until I need you tonight for some more good pussy then you might as well come with me." "O you must be picking Brandon up," she says in a mesmerized voice. Forgetting how it would look that she just did what she did. To her if men could do it then so can women. Shouldn't be no double standard in the world in her eyes. They get to the car and he decided to drive his old school as he caught her gold digger thoughts in her reaction. 1971 Chevy Caprice convertible. His granddaddy always talked about how old school cars was easy access to getting head while driving because it's a bench seat instead of how the new cars are all center consoles or bucket seats. She thought she was getting in the Mercedes S 600. He crunk that 502 engine up carrying 1100 horse power and to her surprise it growled turning her on. They get in the car and start their journey. "O how I love old schools. Come help me out with this," he says while taking his dick out. She looks at it and started laughing. In a pretty, flirtatious voice she says, "Dayuuuum, you might be a bitch dream come true. Can still get hard after all that you just did in the house? He grabbed the back of her head with a fistful of hair and bringing her closer to him while directing her head to his hard dick. She opened her mouth and took his dick to the back of her throat with a small gag. She came up and moved his hand off her head and said, "UnUn. Wait a minute." She tied her long hair up herself and told him while sexually smiling at him, "Nigga you better not wreck or stop me. Since you want it. You better take it like a man. Cause mama not stopping til I get that nut up outcha. "Less talking." "While I show you what a real one can do unlike them lil girls you been dealing with." Jerria went back down on every inch of his dick to gag. Knowing her mouth will produce more saliva. She came up on it slow from the side of it with her tongue sliding on it while her lips still attached to it. Giving the feeling to him a slippery one along with the warmth of her breath alone with the softness of lips.

"SSSSSSSSS" "Keep your eyes on the road, "she says with a mouth full of a dick as she hears his grunts and moans His moans turned her on. She folded her lips over her teeth and sped her head thrust up. Then she started moaning and not slurping because she wanted the saliva to pour out of her mouth while she used both hands to ejaculate him with a twisting motion. Her mouth was serving as a suckulation of his pulsating head. Lucky, he came to a light because she got every drop of sperm out of his as he sat. Beeeeep Beeeeep Beeeeeep. People behind their car started blowing they horns when the light turned green. She never broke stride, and it got better as she knew she made him come to a complete stop and couldn't drive because of how good she was on him. "O my muthafucking God girl. Shit," words he screamed as all his seeds left his body in her jaws. She jacked all of it and held the last jack of his dick up squeezing the last drop out of him firmly. He had a bottle of water on the seat from yesterday and she used it to rinse her mouth. She took the water in her mouth and opened the door and spit his semen out. "Now you got kids on Lee Hwy that you are about to abandon as soon as you pull off," she said with a seductive grin while letting her hair back down. They continue to the airport but the whole time Ricky is in a soul taken daze while driving.

Kim was at home because she didn't have to work today. She was texting multiple guys feeling they heads up with fantasies. Slowly eliminating her candidates because of their lack of spending power by throwing things in the air. Telling one guy she wants a louis Vuitton bag. Telling the other about the cost of a trip and others about things she wants while she entertains their hunger for her. She was also texting the landlord and he had just texted back saying he would accept her offer. "Dam if I knew his old ass was crushing on Big Kim, I would not have been paying him no rent. Dam I slipped," she says lightly tapping her forehead. He texted her and said, "I will put a rush on everything since its cash. Everything will be final on the 24th. Is that okay with you." "Yes," she texted back saying. By that time, Brandon Jerria and Ricky was walking through the door. "What's up lil sis, "Brandon says to Kim as she walks over to give him a hug? "What's up Kinfolk?" Junior says to Kim. "How you doing Ricky? Come give me a hug boy" she says letting Brandon go and walking over to Ricky. She seen Jerria behind the two mountains of men. Jerria and Kim looked at each other. They let the men get in the house and Kim asked her friend, "Bitch do I even want to know how you in the car with them" Jerria rubbed her fingers together signaling money while licking her tongue out. Kim eyes got big as she laughed and asked, "Girl which one?" "Yo cousin. And girl he a real handful." She tried to keep going, but Kim cut her off holding her hand up saying, "Girl he, my cousin. Spare me the details." While laughing at her homegirl, Jr went and got the remote and flipped the tv to SportsCenter. Kim walks over to her brother and says, "Brandon, you owe me one big bruh. The landlord agreed, but he said I have to go on a date with him." "So, what you say" "Well in my head I will be able to spend some of that money that I know he guaranteed to get. I'm just looking at it like my commission. He old and white so he probably on shit that don't even desire fucking." "Sis, I don't want to hear none of that. If you a freak just say you a freak," he says laughing hard as she hits him in the arm playfully. "Linda not gone be the only one getting a commission on the deal. She my homegirl so I'm gone let her get the commission, but me going on a date is only right I make him give me something. He has no idea what he is getting himself in to." Ricky interrupts them and asks Brandon, "Bruh when we gone start trying to build some businesses for the family. I'm sick of buying jewelry and clothes. We need to do it together fam. It will mean more. It means we give a fuck about each other because yes, we both have the money to do whatever we want to do individually but looking out for each other is always better." "I'm ready now wholeheartedly. I'm closer to retirement anyway. And you still have years to play so it will be perfect timing on both sides. I will have to do something after retirement, and you will have something already working for you when you retire." "I already got the Exclusive Sneaker shop doing good as hell. That shit hit bigger than I thought it would." Kim leaned over to Jerria and whispered, "Girl if you wanted to play somebody, you should have waited on my brother. Ricky plays with bitches' mind. My brother doesn't give a fuck just like you." "All money the same money and I'm not Ricky girl so if I fuck his cousin then I fuck him. Shid this my pussy. Besides. All men are similar. It's cool when they do it." "Nah I can't say that. I got a lot of real men in my family, and I actually listen to them, but go on ahead and play with fire. Don't say I didn't warn you." "Warn me of what" "Bitch I know you still about to shoot at Brandon after you fucking Ricky. Ricky not gone say anything, but his action gone show you. He the angel but got a lot of the devil in him, but people forget that the devil was an angel. The shit he do to prove a point I would stab his ass." "Ummmm, I love me a toxic nigga. Bitch u better stop talking cause you are turning on even more." "Look don't treat every man like a trick because everyone don't deserve access to you." "And what that mean because in my eyes, all these niggas' tricks to the right woman." "Exactly. Most men look for the right woman to take care of. That's not tricking. That's being the head of a family. Now treating a man that's looking for the right woman like he a trick is not good." "Aww u think highly of your cousin and that's sweet. But that lil sweet lil dude over there offered to pay a week's pay for me to take today off so he can fuck on me. I'm sorry I got him in my web but I'm bout to drain em because that sound like tricking to me," Jerria says seductively biting her lips and moving her finger down her shirt. "Well, I guess you a hot girl ain't cha." Ricky and Brandon get done talking business and go sat in the living room. Jerria starts her assault on trying to get Brandon attention. Extra slick looks. Batting her eyes at him. Playing close attention to everything he says. Laughing at things that weren't even jokes. "Aye my guy. I need me a car for the time being, but I can't be riding in anything." "Shid you can drive one of mine while you here." "Nah I appreciate the offer, but you know I need my own wheels my guy. While I'm at it, drop me off at the Mercedes dealership my guy. I'm about to lease one or shid depending how I feel I might just buy that muthafucker." "I wish I could be the girl of a nigga with those type of options." Kim and Brandon looked at each other in a playful face as to be asking each other what is she on? Jr. heard what she said and how she said it and shook his head. He got off the couch and went and sat at the house island bar. "Come on big bruh. I will run you down there really quick. Kim, can you take her to get her car." Kim started laughing and say, "Yea. I got her." "I thought we had plans. My stuff still over there." Ricky throws Kim his house key off his key chain and tells Kim, "Big cuz can you go in there and get her bag for her." "Yea kinfolk." Jerria in a pleading tone tries to talk saying, "But-------" he quickly cut her off and said, "But nothing. No foul on the play. I served my purpose and you served yours. Agreement. A bruh I'm in the car, "he says looking at Brandon going to his car. Brandon gives his sister a hug and tells her and Jerria, he will see them tonight.

Linda was having a good day so far. It was 1pm and she had closed on two houses this morning and was showing a potential third one.

"This house sits in the middle of St. Elmo. The property value is high because it is now registered as a historic area. It's an old house but has been upgraded to a modern look. It is located minutes from a lot of tourist attractions such as The Incline, The Aquarium, Rock City, Ruby Falls, and a host of other attractions for families to do. The prestige Howard High School is also located as a zoned school for the kids in the area and with it being a level 5 school academically meaning the highest level in the state, which I'm sure you appreciate knowing that information knowing your kids will be in good hands. This is a five-bedroom three-bathroom house that sits on a half-acre of land. The asking price is $415,999. I will advise to move fast because I have six more showings and one offer on the table." She was showing the house to a couple that was moving to Chattanooga from Alabama. The husband is a lawyer and the wife had just accepted a top position at Tennessee Valley Association. They were black, mid 30s, four kids and down to Earth. Maybe a little bit to down to Earth for some people. The husband asked his wife, "Baby do you like it?" "Yes! I love it! It remains me of my house that I grew up in just with modern designs. I have a question for this sexy woman though," the wife says turning directly towards Linda. "At that price. Your commission is I think six percent right. I think that's around north of a twenty thousand commission check right." Both women gazing in the air as if they were working a math problem out. Linda started nodding yes and say, "Yea I would say that's somewhere around twenty-four to twenty-five large." "Now woman to woman, if my husband was just a man you met in the street, do you feel you would make a move on him." Linda is shocked by the question and checks the wife facial expression to see what kind of test the question was because she definitely did not want to mess up that commission. She was completely thrown off guard though, but she answered and said, "Ummmm I respect marriages, so if I did make a pass at him it would be short lived once he told me he is married or that I recognized his ring." "Well, that's very respectful, but you are telling me if he was offering to compensate you for your troubles you wouldn't take him up on his offer. I think the street term is, if he was willing to trick off, "she asked her with seduction in her voice while standing in a stallion pose. She stood 5'10 with measurements of 38 double D bra size, 34 in the waist, and a size 44 in the ass. A whole lot of women with it being intact in all the right places because she works out. Linda again looks at her and thinks to just show that she is a good girl and don't break relationships up and says, "No. I make enough money where I can trick on myself. A man is just a plus in my life. I would respect you as his wife and not accept anything from him." The wife looks at her and tells her husband, "Baby lets go." Linda looked at both of them in a lost face. She paused for about ten seconds and when they got to the door Linda yelled, "Wait!" Linda put her head down and then looked back up with a lot of confidence and professional sass and continues saying, "Yes." "Yes what?" "Yes, I would have tricked him out of whatever I could get out of him." "Okay now we are getting somewhere so we can talk business." The couple grabs hands and the wife continue, "Let's see then. Since both of us are about to cash you out. We will put an offer in for the full price today depending on you." "What you mean depending on me," Linda says in a lost voice tone. Linda was starting to get curious of where this conversation was going. Little did Linda know, the couple actually requested her. "Well, I say depending on you because I don't like the fact that my best friend is about to give you twenty-four thousand or whatever it is and not receive anything. That's more than a trick off night or week would even add up to." Linda start laughing as she starts getting comfortable and says, "Well that depends on what he was willing to buy because girl as a woman of I can quickly run a tab up," the women laugh and give each other a playful high five. The wife quickly interrupts the laugh after the high five and says, "But what if my husband wanted some pussy," there was short pause then the wife continued and added, "Or better yet. What if I wanted you?" Linda eyes were looking back and forth in between them with the look of a kid in an assessment test trying to pick the right answer. Her multiple test question in her head was the decision of feeling they got her fucked up, these mufuckers crazy, or if she was turned on by the bluntness and kinkiness. "Look baby we bout to make this easy right now. Call and submit the offer to whomever you submit it to and once they call back and accept it, just handle me and my husband." Linda looked shocked and said, "O you mean right now." "What better time than the present my love?" Linda shook her head with a grin on her face but called and put the offer in. They wait and just as the couple thought, the offer was quickly accepted. Linda got off the phone call she had just received and gave the couple confirmation. The three adults smiled at the good news and the wife said, "So this basically our house right." "Yes, I can say that. Of course, we have to sign documents, but" she stopped talking because once she said yes its theirs, both of them started kissing each other and removing they clothes. From the moans and slow touching and the wife telling her husband thanks, it kind of turned Linda on by her surprise to look at love in rare form. Love with no jealousy was actually a site to see. The wife stops kissing her husband and strips him naked. Linda was impressed with his length and smiled but nervously stood there as the wife walked over to her. The slowly grind against her. Seducing her with small touches and sexual talking. Linda is at the moment a virgin being directed by her first experience but slowly beginning to want it. The is naked in front of Linda and is making her rub on her soft body and the husband gets behind her with his hard chiseled body but he is poking her ass cheeks with his rock-hard dick. He turns Linda around and says in a low baritone, "Pick your pleasure." The wife turns her back around and says, "Nah, she don't have to pick. I'm gone let you please her while I let her, please me." They both remove Linda clothes sexually with aggressive passionate touches and kisses. The wife whispers in Linda ear, "Baby I like my pussy ate slow. And even though this will be the first time doing this, eat my pussy the way you want yours ate," the wife demanded. They all went to floor. The wife on her back with her legs open, Linda in between her legs with her ass tooted up while the husband slow stroked her deeply. Moans of pleasure filled the house. All 3 gave each other exploding orgasms and afterwards, Linda playfully expressed to the wife, "Girl I appreciate y'all services but don't try to kill me if he wants some of me again." "Then it will be arranged because I might want some of that mouth again or want to return the favor" Linda didn't expect that response, but nothing should surprise her at this point. After that acquaintance they didn't have to shake hands. They smiled and Linda got out of there and went home and took a shower. She got out and called Post Pro Realty and told them she had to run home. She went to take a shower after her day. The wife texted and said, "Mrs. Linda you was worth every penny. Nice to meet you. Maybe you can show us around since we are new to the city." Linda texted back, "Don't mind at all."

Shante was at work tending to her business. They weren't crowded today like usual. Shante and a girl named Leena handled the load that Jerria left. Jerria texted Shante what happened this morning with Jr. Giving her full detail. Shante told her she missed work on an easy day. A family of three was next in line for Shante to help. A single mother and two kids. Both boys. "Number 74", Shante yells out for her next person in line. Both boys are ten and eight years old. The mother hears her number and tells the boys, "Come on kids. Sit down and just pay close attention." Both kids say, "Okay mom." Shante greets the woman and the two boys as they get to her workstation. "How are y'all today? You boys grab y'all a sucker if y'all mother don't mind." "Thank you", they said as they mother gave them the approval. "Mrs. Stevenson. I called you in because you submitted your tax returns. I see you got married in February. Let me say congratulations for that. Also, congrats on the pay raise that you received, but do to those two things changing, we have to cut you off your benefits with the state. I'm sorry because I see that your husband hasn't brung in any income." Mrs. Stevenson is thirty-two years old. Dark skinned, pure milk chocolate. 5'8 150lbs toned body, dark brown eyes, dreadlocks. She looked at Shante with a scrunched-up face and asked, "So why you sorry?" "Oh, I didn't mean it with no disrespect, but us women always gets the short end of the stick." "All depends on how you look at," Mrs. Stevenson squinches at the name tag and says, "Shante is it." "Yes" "My husband is a man and not a little boy. As my boyfriend, he put me through school for four years with his bare hands and brains. These two boys are not even biologically his, but he is all they know. I am a licensed Nutritionist and because of him I am able to run my own physical training. When you add the internet to it, you can basically say I run a national business. I knew coming in that I would not be getting any assistance anymore and I want to add that the company on file that pays me is my company. I'm an employee of our own business and even though he isn't showing any income, can you guess who gave me the money to get all the equipment I have and pay for the professional footage. No banks was lined up to give me any money and you basically have to be pissed poor to get any help from y'all. I'm not by no means trying to make you feel like I'm blowing you up. I'm only letting you know when it comes to my husband, he is the cornerstone to everything this family is about to accomplish. Tell the Govt, I have a man now and I choose him over them any day. Bye Bye." The woman gets up to leave with her kids and shakes Shante hand. Shante sits back down and leans back in her chair swirling her pen thinking of what the woman was just saying. She was proud to see a sister have a man that she could be proud to be with and couldn't help but to think that's how men has to step back up. Giving assurance to they woman instead of leaving everything up to the woman. Shante rocked in the chair and closed the woman file with the state.

May 13th comes and ironically its Friday which makes it a so-called horror day nationally. Rita made advances at Joshua the last couple days and he offered to meet her at the pool hall off Shallowford road at 9pm. He is the old pharmaceutical guy. They flirted with each other constantly. Her whole objective was to get her a 6-figure sugar daddy in her web. Today was her day off so she worked out and shopped around at Hamilton Place Mall. She made sure to get home by 6pm to give herself time to get ready. Once she got home, she called Linda. Linda answered on the first ring. "What's up Rita?" "Nothing much girl. Look, I know its short notice, but I need you to come to the pool hall tonight with me. If you can, get Eve to come also. I'm trying to get there by 9pm." "What are you up to? Your voice sound sneaky as hell right now. Don't tell me you on freak ho time right now." They both laugh at Linda remark. "Girl, I have no comment for you, but I can say that it will be beneficial for whoever comes with me." "Why there though? You can't even shoot pool, so if you trying to impress someone why go to the pool hall?" "Caaauussee bitch. You know a man always wants to feel they taught a woman something. It makes them feel in control. You know I got to stroke the ego to get to the peso." "See that's why you my bitch and it makes yo psychotic ass dangerous." They laugh again. "Okay I will be there, and I will call Eve and make sure she down. She not doing nothing else so she might as well come, but Rita don't have us in no bullshit. Give me some details or something?" "Girl, I will fill you in later. I promise. Now let me get off this phone and get ready." "Bye Girl." 8:30pm hit and Linda pulls up to pick Eve up. She blew the horn twice and Eve came out and got in the car. "Girl don't be honking your horn twice like you my nigga or something." "You brung your sexy ass out on them two honks like you used to it." They gave each other a playful smirk. Eve had on an outfit from Wet Seal clothing store. Bermuda short blue jeans that hugged her thighs. A half fitted white shirt to show her flat stomach along with her perky breast. Linda had some black jeans and a midnight blue woman's tank top that was from

Wet Seal also that showed her sculptured shoulders and arms. They drive to the pool hall to meet Rita. They got there at the same time. Rita wore some yoga pants that hugged her lovely frame. Rita made sure she showed abs and her sexy v cut that she possesses. A black shirt from BEBE that she tied up in the back to show off her nice plumb booty. She didn't leave no room for imagination. As they walked in the building, they caught everyone eyes. They showed their identification and started immediately complaining about the cigarette smoke. They got their table and Rita made eye contact with Joshua. He was with four other guys. He already had Rita and the girls a table reserved so isn't wasn't any hassle for them to get comfortable.

Linda sees Joshua and leans into Eve and says, "The guy with the plaid button down right there is Rita's mark. I have never seen the other four guys, so I guess it's all fair game on the other ones." Linda nods her head. He reserved they table by their table. Once they spotted the girls had made it in, three of the men left the pool tables to go over to introduce themselves. "Hi ladies. I'm William. This is Jake and Clifford. We just want to tell you that tonight you don't have to reach into your pocketbooks for anything tonight. The pool table next to ours is reserved also for you ladies. Do any of you know how to play?" Eve answers and says, "No. Not the slightest lil bit. I am a great student though. Are you going to give me some pointers here shortly?"

Eve was being her normal self. Her body movement, tone of voice, smiling and laughing, is always mistaken for her to be interested. All three guys were instantly turned on and was about to start a competition for her. They didn't know that she is the one that will take them for everything they got and not have a care in the world. All three women walked over to the tables with the guys and Rita hugged Joshua for them to acquaint each other as they started to chat. "Hey there beautiful." "How is my favorite and only cowboy?" "Well, I'm over here wondering can you handle long objects in your hand?" "I think I got my doctorates degree in doing so," she says while rubbing the pool stick up and down like she is stroking a manly tool. "Unnnn. Y'all nasty," Linda says while laughing and playfully tapping Rita back. Linda comes from behind Rita and says, "And while she is being rude. Hi! Linda and this is Eve. We already met everyone else." Before Joshua said anything the guy, he was playing with came from behind him and says, "How you doing? My name is Buddy. And before you ask, yes Buddy is my name. Buddy Frazier to be exact. What are you ladies drinking tonight?" Eve answers and says, "Well I will take a long isl-----," Linda cut her off and says, "We will take two beers please." "Okay ladies. Coming right up." "Girl, I wanted a long island tea." "And you know how them long islands be having your acting. I'm not about to let you show your natural ass in here around these people we do not know. I will let you do that in familiar territory. With your freaky ass." BJ came back with them two pitchers of beer for they own table. Joshua and Rita went to their own table away from the gang. "Rita, you do know I am married right." "Of course." "So how would this work?" "First off, this is not anything. Yet anyway. I like how you are straight to the point though." "Baby I'm fifty-one years old. No need to be a kid or act like I'm dumb." "Have you ever been with a Black woman?" "Yes! Have you ever been with a white male?" "No. I can't say that I have." "What girl! You don't like creamer nor milk in that coffee of yours," he says in a playful voice. "I never was around enough white boys growing up for me to have a white boy that I was crushing on enough to give them some pussy." "Again Rita, I am fifty-one and don't have time to be playing dumb. You by far the sexiest woman ever approached me from the standpoint of just looks only. I'm realest. It's evident you are looking for someone to as you would say spend a bag on you. Isn't that what you young ins call it these days." "I mean people call it whatever they want to just to feel comfortable with the situation, but everyone knows what it is. Me. I just want to have fun and spend money while having fun." "Well, my girl. I have no problem with it, but my wife will have to sign off on it." Rita was shocked just as Linda was earlier in the week. "See my wife has Lupus and she allows me to have a girl of her approval. She knows my heart is hers as well as my body.

She also is not selfish. She loves me enough to say since her body won't allow her to be sexually involved, she gives me full permission as long as I include her in the process. I have no choice but to respect that level of commitment to me. Her sacrifice for my pleasure is worth full respect of her wishes, so if you want me or anything regarding me, then you have to get her approval first." "And that works for y'all? I mean she doesn't every now again throw it in your face. It seem like that will be to toxic for me." "No disrespect, but that seems to be a black folk's problem or people who comes from poverty. To be frank with you, the media actually wants you all to act like that, but we not going to get into all that." "I bet you wouldn't let her do it if the tables to give them some pussy." "Again Rita, I am fifty-one and don't have time to be playing dumb. You by far the sexiest woman ever approached me from the standpoint of just looks only. I'm realest. It's evident you are looking for someone to as you would say spend a bag on you. Isn't that what you young ins call it these days." "I mean people call it whatever they want to just to feel comfortable with the situation, but everyone knows what it is. Me. I just want to have fun and spend money while having fun." "Well, my girl. I have no problem with it, but my wife will have to sign off on it." Rita was shocked just as Linda was earlier in the week. "See my wife has Lupus and she allows me to have a girl of her approval. She knows my heart is hers as well as my body.

She also is not selfish. She loves me enough to say since her body won't allow her to be sexually involved, she gives me full permission as long as I include her in the process. I have no choice but to respect that level of commitment to me. Her sacrifice for my pleasure is worth full respect of her wishes, so if you want me or anything regarding me, then you have to get her approval first." "And that works for y'all? I mean she doesn't every now again throw it in your face. It seem like that will be to toxic for me." "No disrespect, but that seems to be a black folk's problem or people who comes from poverty. To be frank with you, the media actually wants you all to act like that, but we not going to get into all that." "I bet you wouldn't let her do it if the tables were turned." "Who is to say before the health problem that she wasn't the one that brung men in, but again, that's between me and her. What works for us is for us? Moral of the story is nothing moves without her?" "Well as you just said, to be frank with you, this that white folk's shit." He laughed at her comment and took a drink of his glass of beer with a somewhat half chug. They got up and went to go play pool. Of course, she played her cards right and let him control teaching her how to play. Playfully letting him get her in position and poking her soft ass cheeks against him and rocking as to slight tease him but making sure he feels in control. Eve cannot shoot pool to save her life but oddly she can throw darts. She was on the other side of the bar betting the men on dart games. She had won around five hundred dollars in the short-lived night. They didn't understand she hadn't taken no drinks of beer yet, she was drinking water, so her vision was spot on. "Boys I am going to spare y'all and just go back to my table because I am starting to believe y'all just going easy on me." They do an uproar and say, "Nooo keep throwing." "I might come back then." She goes back to the table and put the money in her pockets. Rita and Linda see Eve going to the table and they both meet her over there. "These white boys' fun," Eve says to the girls. Rita still kind of shocked at the proposal and says, "Yea they fun alright." "Well look. We got to keep them interest, so let's go. Call Jerria and tell her we bout to pull up," Linda tells them. Rita texted Joshua and lets him know she is about to head out and is ready to meet his wife as soon as he can arrange the encounter. Linda walks over to Buddy and says, "Nice to see you. I hope I get to meet the real you next time." "I hope so, but why are you leaving. It's not even 12 o'clock." Linda tilted her head and said, "Well I'm a good girl. I'm not about that vampire life." "Me neither. They bite. I lick gently." "Boy you better stop getting fresh with me before I see how gently you talking about," she says while smiling in a light blush. BJ took a gulp of his beer and humped his shoulders and said, "What you prefer? Your backseat or the restroom and I don't need anything in return." "So that's what you on. I see I am not ready for you yet. Let me grow up a little bit more before I get myself in trouble. Bye my friend." "Bye Bye!" The girls leave and head to Shante them house.

"Man, Michael Myers cannot be human. There is no fucking way this nigga just keeps escaping death. At this point it is not even scary anymore. Give that nigga superpower or something," Brandon says to everyone. Back at the house they were watching the Michael Myers saga since its Friday the 13th. Linda, Eve, and Rita come in the house laughing and talking loudly. "Heeeyyyy. Come on y'all. Let us finish this last thirty minutes of the movie and we will leave and let y'all have y'all little girls talk," Brandon kind of loudly but not disrespectful. "Be quite girls. They at the movies, "Linda says in a whisper as they chuckle softly. The movie goes off and Brandon tells them thanks in a playful tone. He gets up to leave. "Well big bruh, I slick need you to sit in on the convo right now because we need male perspective. And since you my big brother, who better than you to give us advice from a man view," Kim says that then turns to the girls and says, "Where y'all hoes been anyway?" "They went with me on what I thought was some sneaky shit, but all the while his wife oversees every move that we will do. Now I don't know if it will be fun. The fact that we not being sneaky takes the suspense away." "Timeout. Matter of fact, I don't even want to know," Kim says. "Well, she confused but I had fun. Them white boys funded me a shopping spree. I played them in darts after I got them drunk. I could tell they were just entertaining me. And I sholl did let them." "Well me. I almost got this pussy ate on site, but we cannot do that with no money being discussed first." "Right girl," they all say. "Feti gets the pussy ready," says Eve. Brandon immediately burst out laughing and says, "Lil sis. Please tell me you do not think like this. I mean you have had men in your life that has told you to not be a dummy for a man but by no means we told you to basically be a high class," Brandon looked around the room before he finished his sentence and decided not to finish. Kim humped her shoulders and said, "Well I'm not as gone as some, because of men like daddy and Uncle Ricky, but I will say it's a big gap in the generations of men. Daddy them generation was hoes by way of wanting multiple women, but a woman cannot say they wasn't taking care of. They were head of household type men. These days for some reason our black men want to be European and not African nor black. They pants are tighter than ours." "But you will attract what you put out. As of right now that's all I will say. I cannot listen to this and keep my respect, but I will say I would like for y'all to be in a room of every walk of life of men. I am having a party next month and y'all definitely need to come, but y'all are young women so by all means have fun. With that being said, who trying to get some Gucci shoes tomorrow since that's what y'all on. I might as well jump in the game y'all playing."

"Excuse you," they all say as if they got an attitude. "Aww hear we go with the fake shit. Y'all just sit here and bragged about not doing anything unless it's some money involved. I offer on the front end and now y'all feel played. Let me guess. It don't count unless y'all are manipulating the situation so that y'all feel like y'all in control. Y'all want a chump. I'm not mad at y'all though, but Kim. I'm telling on you because I know you know better." Eve slowly walks by him and silently flirtatiously says, "What's going on? I got a pair online that we can order right now." "What you mean what's going on? I mean the whole conversation with y'all is basically fucking for gain right. So, I got some Gucci shoes for some pussy." "Throw in a Gucci jacket with it and we on. That's a small fee for the time of your life." "Time of my life. That's what you bringing to the table for me?" "If you want to find out, I will speak to you later on tonight and we will see." "That's a bet then." Rita was still looking like she in deep thought without a clue to an answer to her questions. So, she turned to her girls to see how her situation sounds. "Look y'all. Let me ask y'all something. What would you do if you were married to a man for 15 to 20yrs and you got diagnosed with Lupus? The doctor tells you your body is too weak to have sex. Would y'all allow y'all husband to get sex from an outside woman?" The whole room got quite and put a look on their face as in saying bitch who about to get killed for touching they man. Shante was the first to say something. "Bitch let me guess. This couple you are talking about is white." "Yea they are but I understand it. Not saying I'm that mature to do it but I do understand," says Rita in response. "Well, my husband when I find one isn't touching anyone else. I can't have sex. Shid, he can't have sex. We gone fight this shit together," says Eve. All the girls chimed in with their opinions and it was unanimous that neither one of them would do it. Linda continued the conversation by saying, "Well to get off that. Based on the shit I just experienced, I wouldn't have thought that couple was white. Black people on some shit now also." "Now what your freaky ass about to confess to us. Your shit be kinky. Spit it out," says Jerria.

"Well Rita, I'm going to say that couple is not on some white people shit. They on some they love each other, and it works for them shit. They are about pleasing each other and not the public eye. Um I sold a house to a couple earlier this week that turned out to be as I would call them swingers. The wife told me she felt like her and her husband needed something back for my commission check on the sale. I told them upon the owner accepting their offer that I will get their first house gift. After I said it, the couple laughed at me. I looked at them like what's funny?" Kim looked at her and smiled and said, "Aww shit. This is about to get juicy. What your freaky as do?" Linda had all her homegirls' attention with big sneaky smiles on their faces getting the gossip. "The wife told me after the seller accepts the offer that she wants to watch me, and her husband have sex. Also, she wanted her pussy ate slowly." The girls in the room erupted with laughter and bouncing on the couches hitting the pillows. Eve gets everyone's attention and says, "But hold on. Are you saying you ate some pussy bitch?" Everyone got quite and stared a mud hole in her anticipating her answer. Linda just smiled seductively and covered her face. "Giiiirrrrrlllll. What pussy taste like? Did you like doing it? I can't believe your freaky ass, but umm. Depending on what that commission was. I might say it was just business and you still is not gay," Jerria says. "Welp, I got like a little under 25k off the deal." "Shid a little. Like 24k"

"Yea I would say it's somewhere in the ballpark," Linda she says with play full gestures. Jerria says, "Well baby. I must say I probably would have took them up on that deal also. And if you would have said you didn't do it, we were gone fight." They all start back laughing and chit chatting. The time got away from them and all of them just fell asleep.

4oclock in the morning comes and Shante sneaks to Brandon room and knocks on the door. Brandon opened his eyes and sat up on his elbows. She walked in with her phone and handed it to him. He took the phone and said, "Why are you handing me your phone?" "Open it. You will see that I don't like Gucci. I ordered to two shoes though as you can see. Two heels from

Louboutin." She pulls his boxer briefs down and he was already on steel rod hard. "Umm. All this meat. Look at me baby." He looked with anticipation. "The sooner you press order on the shoes, the sooner that this grown man attached on to your body goes into my mouth," she says with the sexiest teasing voice she could muster out to seduce him. She was wearing a red and pink one-piece gown from Victoria Secret. She gently grabbed his dick and just held it making squeeze grips on her new best boy toy. "You got 15 seconds to get it done baby." He started moving faster. Mistyping the information from looking at her. She had her mouth lined up with his pulsating mushroom dick head letting saliva run out of her mouth landing on him. He got it all ordered and through the phone down by her eyes so she can see the order with the confirmation of it. "Good Boy" she said in a sexual goddess voice while snaking her body with an arch. Saliva was still running from her lips, and she slowly went down and slurped only his head like a real lollipop and didn't come up off of em. "Uuuuuwwwweeee fuck that felt good." He looked down and was even more excited by the gorgeous face that was in his lap. Her throat game performance was in rare form knowing she was stroking a dick worth million. Knowing the wetter her mouth is, the better it will feel to him. She started giving a slow stroke up down motion on his shaft while slurping his dick head with her full luscious lips and moaning while doing it. Her left hand was rubbing on his stomach so she can feel when he double gasped because she knew that meant it was close. As soon as he took a double breath, she put both hands on his dick and ejaculated him continuously with a twist motion but keeping her mouth on his dick so the saliva could still be running and his dick inside her warm mouth. He lifted up as his nut started coming and his moans and grunts sped up as she sped up. "Give it to me baby," she says quickly and got back to her task. He started thrusting rapidly as she opened her mouth wide allowing a freely entrance to her tonsils. She came off of it and jacked it rapidly turning her head sideways looking him in the eyes as his first explosion came out. As his kids was shooting out of dick like lava running down his shaft, she gently went back on his head sucking gently knowing that everything was tender for him. It turned her on as he was trying to get away but wasn't strong enough to move her. She sucked his dick into submission. She had decided in her head that this wasn't just for a trick off. She wanted him for her, so she had to put on a performance. "Stop. Move. You won. I quit." "Nope. Let me get this up and brush my teeth. Be right back. Don't move." She got out of the bed and went to the restroom to wipe her face, brush her teeth, and googled with Listerine. Went back to his room and wiped him off slowly with a warm rag while talking smoothly to him. Telling him that his dick big and she would love to always make him feel loved and wanted. Basically, acting like his dick was a whole nother person. She had Brandon in a trance. She left back out. Went downstairs with another rag that she made cold. Got three cubes of ice and wrapped it in the cloth. Walked back into his room where he was still in a trance. She used the cold as a stimulant. When it touched him, she knew his body would go in shock as she wanted. She acted as if she was a nurse, and his dick was her patient at this time. "I'm going to make this dick cold and get him back warm from my touch. Baby. From here on out. I don't care who you are with or where you at. This dick mine and I am bold enough to claim it. And don't worry. He was about to stand back up. I understand it's my job to turn you on baby." Brandon just gripping the sheets and grunting while shaking his head with thoughts of he can't let her hook him like this, but lord she is putting up a fight and winning. She took one of the cubes out of the rag and straddled him lining her pussy warmth with his rising dick. Everywhere she rubbed the cube she followed with her lips. She sat up and lifted her gown off and off the full visual of her he wanted her badly. She rocked back and forth lubricating his dick from her moist and she leaned forward and whispered in his ear, "Its morning time. Did you think I was gone leave without sitting on this dick. The head was just my gift. Now I want you to tame this pussy." Now Brandon was turned on to the max. He reached over and grabbed a magnum out of the drawer next to the bed and gave it to her. She sat back and rubbed the magnum down his shaft and anxiously squatted on him cowgirl style. She stays on her feet and grabs his knees leaving a view of her fat plump ass jiggling every time she comes down on the dick. *Splat Splat Splat Splat* with her sexy moans are filling the air. He is thrusting up every time she comes down. She squinching her eyes trying to be a big girl and take every inch like a seasoned pro. "Bring yo ass here" He grabbed two hands full of ass and held her in place while he pounded her. He was challenging her to not wake anyone up. She held a lot back but couldn't help some of the big moans that came out and he loved it because he knew he was doing something. She seen his toes start moving. "O this pussy getting to you now isn't it daddy," she says while moaning. She starts gripping his dick with her pussy walls. "O shit baby," he says as he sped up his pumps. Digging in her she says, "Hit this pussy right their baby. Yes, I'm about to cum." Both nutted together and she stayed in the position, and both didn't move. He went soft inside her. She finally got off him after both stopped breathing abnormally. She looked at him and seen that he was basically out of commission and put her gown back on. Before she walked out the room, she got his attention and said, "Don't forget what I said. That dick mines from here on out. I don't care what's going on. When mama calls, you come." He liked the demanding type and now she had him only thinking of her. It was now 5:45am and as she crept out of the room, Jerria was going to use the restroom and they looked at each other. Jerria smiled and made a money gesture and Shante smiled and made a checkmate motion gesture. They silently laughed. "Dam she done got him. I'm slacking on my macking" Jerria says while using the restroom.

Brandon and Ricky met some other guys at the Chattanooga State Community College gym for a couple of pick-up games of basketball. After they finished playing, they sat around and had normal life talks. "Bruh the problem is you. Not the girl. How you gone fuck two of her cousins and one of her friends and expect her to not nag?

You probably been done already left," Odell says to Tyrine. Tyrine lifts his head up as to be questioning them saying, "So Bruh. Y'all trust women? I'm just doing that to have one up. Women to dam sneaky for me bruh. I literally watched my mama cheat on my daddy my whole life. Nigga one time, my daddy caught her and the dude still in the house. The nigga started acting like he was gay and that my mama was fixing his hair, so my daddy didn't pay it no mind. Time goes by and I see this nigga straighter than yellow street lines. I got older and always looked at my mama like she ain't straight for that. Not the cheating part. Having the nigga in our house part is just foul." "Dam your mama cold blooded." "Nigga then I seen my mama go behind my daddy back getting dick picks from one of his friends. My daddy held it in. He fucked off time to time also to though, but my mama never had any dealings with the girls meaning it was nobody she ever had a friendship or any kind of relation. Moms though. She is fucking with the gay dude, the snitch, and the dude that work at the chicken house that's still trying to have a rap career. All the while still speaking and shaking my daddy hand while fucking his girl. That's the fucked-up part." Everybody falls out laughing. "My dad stayed until I was 18. So bruh. I am not the problem. My mama is." Then he started laughing with everyone else. "Lil Bruh. Your upbringing is subconsciously everyone problem depending on how they were raised. I had a friend earlier in life that did not feel a man loved her unless he beats on her, but it scares me. One day he hit her, and she fell busting her head on the stage on the stairs. She died from the impact. She told me one time, she won't leave because he loves her, but it scares him, so he lashes out. Me and her watched her stepfather kill her mother the same way and she followed suit. Sad to say, but she went right into her mother footsteps," Coach Jay Price says to the young guys. Coach Price coaches the Chattanooga State Men and Women basketball team. He has served as mentor to a lot of young men that has come through his program that goes beyond coaching. He always has good men around such as Coach Travis, Lightfoot, Idris,

Mark, Don, Tank, and a couple more guys that gives the young guys a lot of life advice after playing ball. They talk for about an hour, and they all leave. Ricky and Brandon walk to the car in conversation. "So, Jerria," Brandon throws the conversation straight out there. Ricky brushed it off with a shoulder shrug. "Yea you had hit it that day. I could tell from the vibe. Shid I was proud of ya when y'all came and picked me up on the low." "She sexy as hell, but she all about the next come up. That can't be my girl. I might throw her something to fuck again though. I almost played myself, but I will fuck again. No lie fu." They both burst out laughing. "I hear ya kinfolk. My intention was to come home and catch all of em and knock em down one by one. My bait worked yesterday because this morning Shante woke a nigga up with a GODLY nut. Had me down for the count." "Nigga you didn't fight back." Brandon started laughing and said while still laughing, "Bruh. She caught me down bad. I would tell ya about it, but she seems cooler than I thought. I will say, bruh I think I LOVE HER Geeeeee," he says in a playful voice. "Bruh Granddaddy rolling in his grave right now. You better redeem yourself nigga." "Yea like you should have represented with Jerria right." Ricky pulled his phone out to show Brandon the unanswered calls and text he won't respond to. "Yea it's obvious I put it down, but I shouldn't have because it will never grow to anything. Just a notch in the belt. A very sexy notch though. I must admit." "Man, its Saturday. Let's go to Atlanta tonight. Fuck it." "I'm with it. Let's leave around six," Ricky says looking at the time. It was 1 o'clock. "Aight. I will drive my boy. I need to put some miles on this 600 Benz anyway," says Brandon. They agreed and got in their cars and pulled off.

"Fuck. Niggas are just worse'em. Always want something for nothing," Eve says while going through her messages. Eve and Kim were getting their feet done drinking wine at Brittany's Nail Spa. Black owned spot owned by Brittany. Eve looks at Kim and says, "Girl. Listen to these questions I get sent to my inbox on the daily." Eve deepened her voice as she began to speak to sound like a man while reading the messages.

"Heaven's missing an Angel because you're on Earth. Let me taste something Heavenly." She reads off like five more messages in a man voice and they laugh at all of them. "These dudes going out sad. That's six messages from random dudes just offering to eat a bitch pussy. I mean dam. Is that's what's going on in the world," Eve says with a scrunched-up face. Kim rolls her neck and says, "Girl a nigga told me he will cash app me one hundred dollars for a nude pic of my titties. And they wonder why we look at them like we do. You just read six messages and neither guy asked anything normal. Hi, May I take you out? Hi, May I have a conversation with you while we walk along the bridge? Nope! They jump straight to some fucking shit." The girls that were doing their feet started laughing. They names are Lenzie and Brittany. "Um excuse me. Not to interrupt y'all conversation, but I hear this every day and you two are the first to complain. In my eyes, the men are just going with what's on the menu. The women are the ones that's going out sad," says Linzie. "Right. Just this month alone I've been just shaking my head at these women coming at here. One girl came in here bragging about fucking a dude just to get her nails and feet done. One girl bragged about a lousy seventy-five dollars that a man gave her to fuck. I mean these girls are going out sad. I mean the craziest thing I done heard was a girl saying she wanted to smoke so bad that she gave a nigga some for a gram of exotic weed and a sprite,"

Brittany said while shaking her head but not breaking stride in her task of professionalism of doing her client feet. "You got to be kidding me. So, it's the hoes making it hard for the women. Because there is a difference," Eve says while all 4 women give each other womanly acknowledgement. "Girl. Pssst. Stop judging them and start giving them game. Y'all hoes, including me, are just more expensive hoes. Its levels to this shit," Kim says to Brittany and the girls. "Y'all crazy, but we should start a private podcast for our young ladies out here and just keep it real with them. All kinds of opinions from people from different walks of life. To me the only hoes that should be fucking tortured is the ones going after millionaires and holling that fake rape shit. I hope them hoes burn because being raped is a very traumatizing experience. The man deserves more than a fucking pay out. They should rot in hell. They basically getting away with it because them hoes just want some money. Not to be on anybody side or go to deep with it, but they only doing this to high profile black men. But we are not going there today," says Linzie passionately. They chit chat until their feet were done. They pay the girls and since Brittany is the owner, so they gave her a tip for still blessing them with her professionalism to still work. Eve and Kim head back to the house in East Brainerd. When they got there, everyone was gone. "Kim. I need a favor from you," Eve says while fidgeting her fingers and talking in a voice as to not really want to say anything. "Yea girl. Anything. What's up?" "Well, I never wanted to go to Myrtle Beach. The water is too salty and cold. Wind be high and the attractions are not up to par. Please let's change it to Miami. I know it's late notice, but they will do it for you," she says alluding to the other girls agreeing to change the destination. "You wait until everyone leaves to say this. You could have said this last night or this morning." "Come on girl. Tell me you wouldn't want to be in Miami rather than South Carolina? It's a no brainer for me." "We know that. It's crazy how much Shante knows you. That same day I told her that I would rather go to Vegas or Miami. The other girls already know because they looked at their plane ticket destination. Evidently you didn't and Shante bet all of us that you weren't because of your little spoiled attitude," Kim says and laughs. Eve pulls her flight up in her email and sure enough the destination clearly says Miami. "Fuck y'all. I'm not near spoiled. Y'all just love me," Eve says licking her tongue out like a playful little kid. "Girl if you weren't spoil, you would have been looked at your ticket, but you secretly kept a spoiled attitude. Now, I got to buy Shante a bottle at the club for losing the bet on your spoil behind." They both laugh and Eve tells her, "Girl, I will split it with you." She starts twerking while Kim was tapping her ass saying, "Ah ah ah" "Yeap. Miami about to get E.V.E. The Chattanooga edition.

Linda looks at her phone and sees she has a text that she hasn't read. It was the married couple asking for a bar for them to go to this Saturday. Linda sent them five spots that she thinks they would like. She was at Hamilton Place Mall in the Victoria Secret Stroe. As she walked out of the store she almost collided with a guy by the name of Mike. "Woah! Excuse me," as he stopped on the dime to avoid collision. "No that's my bad. I'm walking with my head down looking at this phone not paying attention." Mike looked at her with eyes of a predator that spotted his prey. She had on white shorts with a lime green and white shirt from The White House Black Market women clothing store. She was showing off her thigh tattoo. Her legs were perfectly shaved with baby oil on them that had her legs glistening. She also sized him up quickly. He was normal. He had on black Levi Jeans, a black shirt, and Jordan #4s black. What she noticed was that the shirt was fitted to his chest and arms meaning he worked out. Also, the watch he was wearing was a Submariner Rolex. A fifty grand or more timepiece. Just so she could get a better view," she asked, "I was looking to see what time it was when I was looking down. Can you tell me what time it is please?" She was lying. "O it's just 3:30, but what's your name." "Hi! My name is Linda," she says extending her hand out for a handshake. He accepted her hand and lightly shook it and then asked, "So miss Linda. Who got your attention that you almost colliding with people because there is no way you were looking for the time. That's a quick glance to check. With me liking what I see, I hope it wasn't you texting a significant other or anything like that." "If I had a man that had my attention like that, I wouldn't be standing in front of you giving you my attention because that would be disrespectful to him. I wasn't raised like that." Her comment immediately made the hairs on the back of his neck stand up at the fact she knows how to handle herself if she had a man in the presence of another man. "Well dam that sounded good and it's nice to know that women with that mind frame still exist. This was fate." "O it was huh." "Got to be. And I'm sorry. I'm Mike. I was in a daze." "Well Mike. Goodbye!" "Nah. It's see you later. I am going to make sure I see you again." "O is that right." "Definitely." They part ways and of course Mike watched her ass cheeks and legs as she walked off. She put on an extra twist to give him a show also. She walked through the food court to one of the restaurants named Red Robin. They're famous for their burgers. She walked in and seen the guy she was meeting. She purposely didn't take her bags to the car. She was hoping she could stroke his ego and get him to reimburse her on her gifts to herself. The guy she is meeting name is Jared. A street hustler that spends more than he makes and can't figure out why his money won't grow. He had on a Born fly fit Detour Clothing. A male urban clothing store in the mall. She got to the table and gave him a slow kiss. "Baby I've missed you. I haven't stop thinking about you since our last close encounter. You almost had me with your slick self," she says while playfully hitting him on the shoulder. She sat her bags down and they both sat down. The waitress comes over to get their order. "May I take y'all order?" "Yes! Could I get some buffalo boneless wings and ranch sauce. An Arnold palmer to drink with an extra lemon please." Linda looks at Jared and says, "And he will like the Roy'all Burger meal and a coke." The waitress looked at him to confirm and he shook his head yes. "Okay. I will be back with your drinks. "I see you had fun in the mall," he says looking at her bags. "I didn't have enough money to finish. Victoria Secret got these two-night gowns I would have liked to get. I couldn't get any heels or thigh boots. I also need my LeCoeur make up line products. Shit. I forgot to get me a bathing suit." She changed her voice to sexy voice and says, "But baby. You know what I didn't forget no matter what I wasn't able to get for myself." "What's that?" She hands him the Footaction bags. It had the new Jordans and two sweat suits to match the shoes. "I didn't forget someone that's important to me." That little gesture dropped all his defenses. The waitress brung their food out along along with their drinks and a refill pitcher. "I appreciate it. How did you get a raffle ticket though because I know your little boujee self don't know anything about that." "Well, little do you know. Boy I'm slick the plug. Plus, I knew how bad you wanted them after how mad you were that you didn't win the raffle, so I pulled my little strings." "Well look at that. Just when I want to try to complain about something, you come through in the clutch for me." "What do you want to possibly complain about," she says in a little spoiled girl voice as she moves from across from him to his side of the bench. She starts slowly playfully seducing him with touches of his thigh and shoulders. Instead of taking quick sips from the straw she would slowly fundle with the tip of the straw with her tongue with a swirl before placing her lips over the tip to make his mind fantasize as if it was his manhood going in her mouth. She knew she had his full attention. Instead of letting the straw go she slides it out of her mouth slowly. She hadn't fucked him so everything she did was a wish for him, and she knew it. In his mind, she was a good girl that he was going to have to work for. Now in her mind, she wasn't gone never fuck him anyway. Just an atm machine to her if he was willing. He looked at her and slouched in the bench seat and said to her, "It's been over a month and you still fronting on me." "You must be talking about sex. I told you. You can't put time on something that once you get it, it will change your life. Plus, you couldn't possibly think just buying me things grants you access to heaven. If you want some pussy that's special, then you must do something that's special. Make me feel like it's me and nobody else." He took a bite of his burger and thought about what she had just said while chewing. She moved back to the other side of the table. As she was moving, he says, "That's not all the way true, but I see your point if this was within the first week or two. It's been damn nearly six weeks. Shid a nigga definitely showing top notch interest." "You must think I'm a naïve female or something. Luckily, I had a father in my life that gave me a set of rules. For One, I haven't been introduced to anyone in your family. That means I'm nothing that you look at as long term in your life. Two, you saying it has been six weeks and this the closest thing we been to a date which means you too busy for Linda. Third, gifts get you attention and flattery points. Not pussy. I am not going to keep going because I feel like I will be giving free game. I will lastly say, I'm not a female out here living without things that I hope a nigga replace for me. The man that swims in me will gain a plus one to his life and not a liability." The confidence she spoke with was what Jared was intrigued by about Linda. He tries to fire back and says, "Man all that sounds good until you asking me for something." "Um correction. I haven't asked for anything sir. You have offered everything you have ever gave me and you be compensated in the same fashion. Not as much but you definitely get things also. Then you must think I'm dumb or something. You been working on your old school car for 6 months right." "What does that have to do with anything that we are talking about?" "Because that lets me know that if you see value in something you won't give up on it. Linda pussy is just like finding a street plug or finishing that Chevelle. My pussy is a prize and deserves to be treated as such. Gifts are a plus, but it doesn't put me in a special seat with you." "What can be more special than getting bands spent on you?" "You are so cute," she says with so much sarcasm. She continues and says, "Let me prove my point. You post a picture every day with your homeboys to let everyone know who your homeboys are right. Post a picture with me right now giving me a kiss and I will fuck you tonight." She moved back over to his seat to challenge him, and he put his head down and chuckled. "So, you got all the sense in the world don't you," he says defeatedly looking back up. "All I am saying is this pussy is as valuable as that car you are posting and putting all that time into, but I don't have to get rebuilt. My value is already in me because no one is touching me. Plus, if I'm yours, I actually add value to you." "You got a way with words I see." "Nah it's just real shit." They finish their food and talking. The waitress comes to ask if she can get them any dessert and they decline. Linda quickly hands the waitress her card to pay for the food. "You don't have to be paying for food to prove you can do for yourself. Awww, you mad at me" he says in a playful voice. "Nah I'm not mad and I don't have anything planned." He reached in his pocket and gave her two thousand dollars. "Nah. Go back in the mall and get the stuff that you missed. That will cover everything you want plus the things you just bought me. With the rest, book us a date of your choice and pay for it in advance." "Look at you trying to take initiative." He seen her face didn't change though. All a game to her though. Plus, she is very observant of her competition and other people motives. She purposely left before Jared knowing that he was showing interest in the waitress. His non ability to not show interest in other women is one of the reasons he will never be able to fuck Linda, but she will always get what she can get. Linda grabs her bags and gives Jared a peck kiss on the jaw. Walks up to the cash registers where her waitress was so she could sign the receipt. "Young pretty girl. How old are you baby girl?" "I'm twenty years old." "With a lot of life ahead. Look baby. Advise from me. Ever since I walked in, I observed you eyeing my bags and with you thinking he bought the bags I seen you giving him extra eye looks and him entertaining it. He not my man. You gone go over there and start cleaning the table off and he is going to ask you for your number. You were gone give it to him as you should because you don't owe me any loyalty. Plus, he not my man, but you can get him to trick off on you. Promise me though. You will not fuck him. Once you do that, he will literally stop talking to you because he would have accomplished his goal. Get what you can out of him, but do not fuck him. He a whole street nigga with no ambition." Both ladies looked over at him and he didn't notice. Linda turns back to the waitress and says, "He's all yours baby girl." The waitress being young minded and thinking the quicker she gives him some is the quicker he spends a bag on her is her mindset. Jared ended up fucking the girl in a week for a phone bill payment and panties. When she tried to get in touch with him the next day, he had her blocked. She was fine though because she had got a free month of phone service in her eyes. She was the type that was making it hard for people.

The next Saturday a guy named Dontae had posted on all social media platforms to bring their cars to him for a good carwash. Dontae was a guy that has a clear entrepreneur mindset. He's thirty-two years old. Six foot five, two hundred seventy pounds and always got something he's trying to do. He's been trying to get Kim attention since they were thirteen years old. She never wanted to be his girl, but they were friends. Quietly, he wanted to succeed so he could have the confidence to try to get at Kim. All the girls were at Rita's house conversating. "So, Rita. What did your freaky ass decide to do with the married couple," asked Jerria? "O girl. I met the woman and everything. Her strength made me respect her too much, so I couldn't do it. I feel I would fuck her husband way to good," she says twitching her hips hard walking to a chair. "Aww.

That's quite mature of you might I say, but how you know that old white man won't fuck the shit out of you," asked Eve? "Girl that old white man ain't had that dick bounced on and cheeks clapping that dick while he nuts. You know white folks got that one motion sex." They all laugh. "But I'm not just all the way out of it because it is still tempting because of the arrangement and I'm single anyway. Kim gets their attention and says, "Girl, you know you about to give in. It's on your mind too much, but shid we not gone be mad at cha at all honey. But look, before I forget, I need all you hoes to follow me so that Dontae can wash our cars. He in the East Lake Boys Club parking lot across the street from East Lake projects." "That boy still around here trying to make something happen ain't he. Shid I'm not mad at him at all. I respect that a lot from anyone," says Linda. They chit chatter and get in their cars to head down to fourth avenue. When they pulled up, Dontae was in great spirits seeing them. He got right to work immediately. The Boys & Girls Club was letting him use the water from their building. As he finished everybody's car, he joined them in conversation. "Ladies Ladies Ladies. I really appreciate y'all coming down here to give me some support. Me and my nephew really needed it. We been out here for two hours, and nobody has stopped." "So why you still that got that baby out there holding that carwash sign like it's some hope in getting some business," Kim asked in a concerned voice for the boy?

"Because he has been giving my sister a hard time. Getting in trouble and stuff." Dontae lowered his voice in a saddened way and continues saying, "He just acting out because of the lack of money he knows that they have. Trying to sell drugs and rob. My sister working 12-hour shifts so she is doing what she can but the way inflation done hit the world, it's hard for her without the help of that fuck nigga that supposed to be her baby daddy. Fuck him though because I decided that I'm going to do more, so I started this cash business and made him my partner. This my way of showing him that it's no excuse to not have things, but you have to work for them and what you don't got isn't a reflection of being poor as long as you happy with yourself. I'm putting self-esteem into him." "How old is he Dontae," Kim asked? "He fourteen." "And at fourteen what were you doing Dontae," she says with sarcasm with her hand on her hip. "Well, that's my point of deciding to do more. Since I done been through what he is going through, I'm the best candidate to help him not go down the same path right." "Right. I'm glad you are looking at it that way." "Remember when I was selling candy out of my locker in high school. Had the blow pops for a quarter, Reese's cup, snickers, Twix, and potato chips. Off the tootsie pops alone I was making a profit." "Yea I was your favorite customer. You gone try to make some money. I got to give you that." "So, him standing out there on that corner is building discipline that he didn't even know he had."

"Welp in my eyes its child abuse because he been out there not attracting any cars to turn in. He out there in that hot sun sweating for no reason. I'm about to call that baby in." As soon as she was just about to yell for him, Dontae looked at her with a stern face and cut her off in a stern steady voice and says, "Look if you don't like what you see you can leave just as you came, but you not interrupting shit that I got going on with my nephew. That's your women problems for today. Y'all baby them for every fucking thing and get mad at the soft ass man they become. If I'm not mistaken, you are literally all your adult life talk about how men not stepping up and not worthy. Well, how in the fuck can they get worthy when the standard is, Baby sit back because mama, aunty, granny, or sister will do it." She tried to cut him off because his voice had risen. Clearly grilling her. "Who you think...." "Shut the fuck up. I'm not done. Listen sometimes and you might learn something. I'm not letting my nephew get conditioned to be catered to by a woman at the expense that he doesn't learn how to provide as a man. He is not gone automatically depend on his girlfriend all because of all the women babied him and now he is looking for that in every woman. Flipside, when he gets out of y'all care, that little girl gone immediately tell him she not his mama and not putting up with that. Y'all crippling these fucking boys. My nephew not gone be like that as long as I'm alive. All jobs don't come with a desk and air conditioning. Didn't get a lot of cars but in 3hours the company made $180 dollars. Now since you have so much concern for him, why don't you walk your smart mouth ass over to him and give him a ten-dollar tip." He had her full attention with eye contact and her mouth open like a little girl. She was hoping one of her home girls was gone chime in and help, but they were at full attention of his words also. When she was looking at them to say something they were turning they head like they not in it, playfully. After he had said take his nephew the money for a tip, she hesitantly took in what he said and turned to walk to the young boy. Dontae sat down and the other girls came over to him laughing and they engaged in conversation. Kim came back from talking to the nephew and with a smart playful little girl gesture she said, "And I gave him a fifty-dollar tip." He laughed and shook his head. He walked to his car and got some paperwork off his backseat. He walked back to them and said, "A before y'all go. I'm taking this carwash thing serious. I wash y'all cars anyway so let's do it professionally for it can mean something to the banks and lending companies. Can y'all sign these contracts stating that we locked in for me to wash y'all cars for this year. The package is a carwash every Friday and one wax per month for one hundred fifty dollars." "Do this include vacuuming, tire shine and interior with the smell good in this price," ask Linda. "It wouldn't be right if I didn't include that in if for y'all," he said. "Well, I don't have a problem with that price. Plus, I respect what you are doing and can fit that in my budget. Also give Kim some more contracts so we can make sure you at least got all six of us under contract." They contracts says they agree to start on June 1st. Dontae walked over to his nephew to explain the importance of contracts. Linda and Kim were talking as they were walking to their cars to leave. "Girl, he got yo big ass right together. I was looking like Kim not gone even say nothing. That's the first in history." "And girl when I tell you that shit made my pussy soaked for some reason. While he was talking it's like it was unlocking something inside of me that just started my juices to flow. Clit throbbing and shit. Girl it just ain't nothing like a man with a backbone baby," Kim says. They give each other a high five after her words and got in their cars and left the scene.

Later that night, they all went to Club Euphoria to just get out and chill. Shante was having herself a good time. She was dancing with people and making the girls get on the dance floor with her. The DJ was hitting all the right songs back-to-back. They went to the restroom as a pack. A rule of theirs since they were eighteen years old. They bought some gum from the bathroom lady and went back and sat at the bar. Men were walking up offering to buy them drinks as usual. Shante wouldn't take any. After she turned down the fifth guy Eve said, "Bitch what's going on? We gotta talk. You must be withholding some information from us or something," she says with a sneaky girl smirk. "Nah. But my attention has shifted to a one person. That's all. Imma just chase him and see if I catch him. He's definitely worth it. He in my trial phase right now." Jerria was about to playfully say she know who it is, but before she was able to fully get everybody attention and reveal what she knew, Shante was already staring at her with bitch shut up eyes. Young Jones came over to make sure they were having a good time. It was his party. Dontae was with him, and he offered everyone drinks. Shante says, "Preciate it, but I've had enough." Of course, Rita, Eve, Linda, and Jerria took him up on the offer. "I'm okay also," says Kim. "Cool. By the way. We're good right," he said with a smile referring to earlier. "Honey yes." He smiled and walked off after they gave each other a light hug. "I think that boy secretly has always liked you girl, but never knew how to come at you," Rita says to Kim. "Psst. I don't think so. Especially with them little chicken head hoes that he be talking to. Ever since we were kids, ain't none of them hoes ever compared to me. Rita sips her drink and put on a smile and said, "Well sounds to me you've been sizing his women up since we were little. Girl let me find out you're slick in the cut." All the girls start laughing. They continue to have a good time and chit chatter. The night ends and everyone made it home.

Sunday morning on the 22nd, the girls met at a restaurant called Scotty's on The River for brunch. "Um Jerria. Shante. I might as well let y'all know now that my brother bought the house, we're living in. Everything is supposed to be finalized this week." Jerria says, "O hell yea. Can you say no more rent payments?" holding her hand up for a high five to Kim. Kim left her hanging and said, "No that's not what that means. We were paying $2500 in rent. Me and Jerria was paying $800 a piece and Shante was paying 9 because she got the big room. He just gone charge us $1500 but on paper he's leaving $2500 so the tax purposes and value." "Well, that's straight. I can't complain about that. Somebody ain't going to be paying rent long now anyway," Jerria says with a sneaky smile glancing at Shante. Kim thought she referring to her, so she said, "Nah girl. I wouldn't play y'all like that nor my brother. Plus, I would prefer giving my brother rent money rather than a landlord I never met. I'm just glad he trying to learn investments that secures him a future." The waiter comes and get their order. He turns their order slip in then returns with their drinks with two refill pitchers because they all ordered Sprite to drink. A guy by the name of Chivas was there eating also with three of his homeboys. He 6'4, 280lb, dark skin, 360 waves, with a mouth full of golds and groomed shaped nicely facial hair. He couldn't take his eyes off Jerria. "Excuse me ladies," he says as he approached the table.

"Um I'm sure y'all get approached a lot, but um y'all friend here," he says pointing at Jerria, "I would like to ask if I could talk to you at the bar for about five minutes? By that time your food should be back." "Well, he was bold enough to walk up to a table full of women. You should see what he has to say," Eve says. Jerria says, "Cool." Chivas leads her to the bar. "This week can't go by fast enough. I'm ready for Miami. I'm trying to find Ross shid," Rita says. "Well, he has a mega mansion in Atlanta so you're looking in the wrong place. Plus, you hoes know y'all should have told me the flights were to Miami. Thank y'all though because I was really dreading the thought of South Carolina over Miami," says Eve. "I bet your spoiled ass was," says Shante as they all chuckled. They keep conversating and Linda looks out the window of the restaurant and says, "O I like his style. He's hustling. This might be the business that works for him." All the girls turn to the window and see Dontae and his little nephew outside in the parking lot washing cars. "Here's y'all food ladies," the waiter says as he hands everyone their order. "Thank you, baby," Kim says to the waiter. "If y'all need anything else just let me know," and he walks off. Jerria comes back smiling and giggling. "So, what was he talking about," Eve asked Jerria? "Well, he's from Atlanta. Played football for UTC and he's currently a promoter. For Father's Day, which is next month, he just locked in Dblock JMac, and Slatt Zy for a concert at the McKenzie Arena.

Tickets go on sale tomorrow," she says with an attitude of a come up. "Well, that's what's up. I take it we are front stage then right." "Now you know this. I got his number. He can stay around for a little while. I heard he gone try to book Future, so I got to entertain his little ego so I can meet Future when that happen. I'm trying to let him fuck me in some Gucci flip flops." The whole table burst out laughing. "Look who I run into while I'm working and networking. Y'all are my good luck charms. Me and my nephew just washed ten cars in the parking lot." "Well, why don't you sit and eat with us? Afterwards, you can pay for our food," says Eve. Dontae laughed and put his hand on his nephew shoulder and said, "Nephew. Always be willing to treat the needy and show appreciation, but when it comes to women. You are only obligated to take care of whom is yours. Now these women are all beautiful, but do they belong to me? Meaning have you ever seen me with any of them out or at the house?" "No Sir." "Well then, I'm not obligated to pay for their food." The women looked and smiled. Then Jerria says, "Unless you get turned out, but that conversation is for when you are older." "See nep, you gotta be on the lookout for pretty women. Make sure they intentions are pure. Come on before these beautiful women corrupt your head. Good day ladies." He walks off with his nephew. Kim gave him an extra friendly look as he walked past her. He noticed it and nodded his head at her. "He might turn that little boy into a man after all. It's sad that more of our young black men don't have a positive influence in their life. I respect him," says Linda about Dontae. "Yea. I respect what he is doing, but at the end of the day he just washes cars," says Jerria. Shante looked at her friend with deadly eyes and said with a clear disgust, "Says the girl who fucked a millionaire and blew it in one day." All the girls looked shocked at Shante. They laughed it off, but the truth always has hurt more than a lie. The girls get done eating and chatting then leaves.

May 26th, they board the plane at 8:00 am and they were ready for Miami. They flew on a direct flight to Miami from Chattanooga. When they got there, they went and picked up the two

Chevrolet Tahoe SUV's they had reserved. Shante got a deal on a mansion off Air bnb. She doesn't know why she booked it, but she was going to make the most of it. She planned to have a small house party since she got the extra space. The girls get there and immediately gets excited. Everyone went live on their social media platforms doing their own version of stunting. "Shante. Um. How much is this? I know I should have asked that question a long time ago. Are you sure the money we put in gone cover this or is we gone owe you something on the backend," asked Rita. "Don't worry about how much it is. The money in the pot is enough to cover it. I just ended up lucking up on a good deal. Got us eleven bedrooms, 13 bathrooms, a state of the arch pool, and a workout area." "Girl I am not mad at cha at all. Shit like this be putting me back in my place. Letting me know I don't have no dam money. It's always another level," says Linda. "I'm about to run to Wal-Mart to get some lil extras for me. Y'all want anything back?" As soon as Rita asked if they needed anything, they all started rambling off everything. Rita quickly cut them off saying, "Nah. Y'all might as well get on up and come on with me. I didn't hear none of y'all and I wouldn't remember all that shit anyway." All of them contested what she said, but knew she was telling the truth. Of course, they gave a lot of lip like only a woman can, but they got on up and they all went on to Wal-Mart. They pull up and Rita says, "O hell yea. They got a liquor store attached to it. I can kill two birds with one stone right now." Wal-Mart was a melting pot with out of towners and the locals. Women were shopping with just their swimsuits on bikini flip flops looking very edible to the men eyes. The men were shirtless with swim trunks and swim shoes. They were definitely not in Chattanooga anymore. They got everything they needed and headed back to their mansion for the weekend. They get there and put they groceries and snacks up anounge in the living room and start talking. "To pop off the weekend, I got a flyer from this dude at the Wal-Mart. Trick Daddy hosting a party tonight at a spot tonight called

Studio 60. The lil dude told me if we wanted a real Miami clubbing experience then that's where we need to be tonight." "So just like at home, we about to be running from shootouts," says Rita. "Nah. Don't get boujee just because we out of town bitch. You the main one choosing the hole in the wall clubs back home. You like that shit. Plus, we got all week to be boujee. Let's fuck with the hood one time while we are here," says Jerria. "Fuck it then. Who on the flyer that supposed to be performing or is Trick old ass still trying to get on stage. He better just be the host because I don't know none of his songs for real for real." They both started reading the flyer together and seen that the flyer just said Trick Daddy and friends.

Shante looks at her phone to google the things that's gone be at the Miami clubs for the weekend and she ran across an old school party that was featuring Uncle Luke. She came across it and said, "A y'all. My mama loves this man. Since we fucking with the hood tonight, lets fuck with the older crowd tomorrow." "Who the hell is Uncle Luke? That's a little too old school. His rap name is Uncle. Man let me look him up," says Jerria. They all get on YouTube, and they recognized songs they done heard and danced to but didn't know that it was an Uncle Luke song. They also came across old party clips that the 2 Live Crew done rocked out. Even seen when he came to Chattanooga a while back. Jerria was all into it while twerking and then said, "It's not my girl Cardi B but that shit lit for some club shit so I'm with it, but after looking at them clips, my mama, aunties, uncles, etc. bet not never say anything about this day and age music. They were freaks also. Shid they might be even freakier. I know I bet not see anything with my mama doing none of this shit I just watched." "Girl hush. All our mamas probably were hoes and if they weren't, they got hoe tendencies. All women do," says Rita. Ricky Jr called Kim's phone in the middle of their conversations. She answered on the second ring, "What's up Jr?" "I'm good. Just landed in Miami and getting my car for the weekend." "That's what's up. We're already here also." "O trust me. Y'all stunting to hard in that mansion y'all staying in. I been seeing y'all live videos." "Shante found it." "Shid, I got some of the fellas that flew in today that play for the Orlando Magic and the Lakers. Shid tomorrow why don't y'all host a day party from like 2pm to 7pm? I can invite the guest. I light lil 75 people. And yes, every nigga that comes will be a nigga that's on his shit." "I'm cool with it. Imma run it by the girls, but I'm pretty sure they gone be cool with it. Let me call you right back with the answer." "Okay cool." Kim gets off the phone and gets everybody attention. "Hold on y'all. Look. Aye!" They all stop laughing and look at Kim. "I just got off the phone with my cousin Jr and he just landed down here." "Nope, Nope, nope. He is not staying here," says

Jerria with a clear attitude. Kim looked at her like she was stupid with a smirk of bitch pipe down. "Um you do know that's my family and if he needed somewhere to stay, he is more than welcome to stay anywhere that I'm at, right?" Jerria rolled her eyes and looked the other way with her arms folded. Kim looked at her with a face that said bitch there is nothing you can do about it either. Kim continued, "Now back to what I was saying before I was interrupted. I just got off the phone with Jr and he wants to know would y'all be interested in hosting a day party here from two to seven pm. He has some people that also flew in and yes, the guys that are coming are probably millionaires or at least making six figures. He didn't say anything about bitches, but he is a man so I'm pretty sure he gone invite some more women." All the girls instantly agreed with the day party with the thought of just pure having fun. Jerria for some reason kept her little attitude, but now in her head she was about to play get back. Little did she know that her plan will do more damage to her image than anything she was planning for the next. Kim calls Jr back and lets him know that they are on. He lets her know that he won't crowd the house but have a nice crowd of good vibing people. A good mixture of personalities. Time past by and they all got ready to go out. All of them looked like video vixens stepping out. They got to the club at 9:30pm so they could get a good parking spot, but it was already packed. "Well dam! When they say doors open at nine then that is what they mean I see," Shante says while driving through the crowds. They were about to experience a Dade County party. They are passing by spots but see the prices and being typical women not wanting to pay the full cost but want a perfect parking spot. "Girl after we come out of the club, I don't want to be walking no dam blocks to get to the dam car. We need to go ahead and split this hundred-dollar car parking. It's 3 of us so that's just thirty-three dollars apiece plus one dollar. Ion know what them hoes gone do," Shante says alluding to the other three girls trailing them. "Well, I am pretty sure it's gone be this way all week so I will just pay tonight and one of y'all handle tomorrow," says Kim. "Okay girl," Rita and Shante say. They pulled into the first parking lot and the guy stopped them for the fee. "Damn beautiful! I think I'm gone have to come in and find you." "Is that so. I will buy you a drink if you find me, but you got to give me a parking spot." The guy was in his late 40s for sure. Haitian and African American, Gold teeth, salt & pepper wick locks, and about 6'1. He looked a little harder and smiled. He responded to Shante and said, "Nah this is business. I can't just give you a spot, but you girls look a little too fancy to be here. Y'all gots to be from out of town." "We from Tennessee." "Aight TennaKey. Y'all actually look a little too young for this party. Have y'all even heard of Quad City DJs or 69 Boyz." "No but it sound old off the mere fact it's a group. I thought the 90s party was tomorrow with Uncle Luke. A guy told us this gone be Miami party." "Well, he right except he should have said a Florida party. Trick from Miami though. I guarantee y'all have fun though if y'all get out but look. You said give you a spot. I will give you a discount if you name a Quad City DJ song." "Why you couldn't say a Trick Daddy song," Shante says while handing him the hundred dollars for parking. He laughed and they proceeded to park. They actually found two spots beside each other so that was good. Each woman stepped out looking like a lottery ticket. "This muthafucker lit, but it looks like it's more older women and men that's gone be here for real. These surgeries done brung Auntie them back cause these old hoes sitting up down here," says Jerria. "They body could be natural. Everybody didn't go on the surgery table, but surgery or no surgery, they are looking good. I hope I look like they are looking when I'm their age," says Eve. The walk to the entrance and the first wave of security that's checking women pocketbooks says, "O yea. Y'all not from here, but we appreciate the lady like look y'all bringing into the building." "It cannot be that noticeable that we are not from here," says Jerria. "Welp one reason that I know is because if you look around, no other women here have on a dress because they know that this party today is a real party. Women dance in here and not just look pretty. They look pretty and dance. Plus, everyone from the city knew who Trick Daddy was bringing as friends. Out of towners didn't. Besides y'all look too young to know some of the songs that's about to be played. My advice is just have fun. I guarantee you want regret it." "Well fun is what we came to have so show us a good time then." One of the studs behind Jerria and her girls spoke up and said, "O I hope you open to cross the track fun," alluding to not being straight and engaging in girl-on-girl activity. None of the girls responded. They just gave each other that girl look as in saying, this bitch better gone somewhere. It was a male and female security that said. "Y'all gone on in and make some memories. They got pat down thoroughly and proceeded into the club. They instantly could tell that they were out of place but could see it was about to be a fun night from the vibe. Wasn't anyone looking for people they don't like or no females arguing over men with vica versa to men. It was just a happy party. Rita and Eve were convinced this is where they needed to be. They also were two out of three with shorts on instead of a dress. "Tonight, is on me ladies. My gift for the weekend," says Linda. She seen that only the VIP line was moving swiftly. "Hold this spot for us y'all. I'm about to go check something. They got me fucked up down here. They here all kinds of men hovering over the lines saying prices that they can get people in for but the girls didn't pay them any mind. As Linda got out of line, she went over to the VIP line. She got to the front and the guy looks up at her, then around her and asked, "Which guy sent you," him alluding who to give the sale to for they cut? Linda responded, "Neither one of them. But me and my homegirls want a floor booth." "Is that so." "Yea. Its 6 of us. And please don't try to treat us like some slow bitches. I heard the price you gave the niggas before me, and I want the booth next to theirs." "Well, if you heard it, you know that its 10k." Linda pulled her debit card out and signaled for her crew to come over. They seen her signaling them and walked over to her. The guy swiped the card and motioned for a security guard to escort the ladies to their section. The DJ was playing everything from 1993 to 2016. The club was rocking. The girls didn't know a lot of the songs, but they couldn't deny the beat and to the songs such as Tela, Do or Die, 12 Gauge, and many more. It was also a cultural shock to them because they were accustomed to standing in packs of women and just twerking while ignoring men, but the women would be chanting and smacking them on their behind. In this party, the women were dancing with the men and the men were circled around the women smacking them on they ass. Another thing, the men could dance just as good as the women. Nobody in the club was like a light pole just standing still. Everyone was interacting and having fun. A man would walk up to the booth and ask for one of them to dance with them. Nothing more or nothing less. Not acting like a scumbag if they said no. Just a good vibe. The guys saluted they bottles and cups to them for being in that certain VIP area because they knew the cost, so evidently those women were on they shit. "Girl these old heads are live at five with no place to hide in this muthafucker," Eve says with a big smile after returning from dancing. "Girl, I wish parties like this existed back at home. I bet our old heads be partying like this. Imma have to check one of the old spots out when we get back to see what's going on in there. If it's like this, Imma have to party with them or even start having parties and making some money on the side, making the age limit 35 and up," Shante says in a slight buzzed from the liquor voice. The guy from the parking lot walks by and says, "Oh I found y'all. I see who the ballers are tonight. I see how y'all do," he says referencing their booth in a playful manner. Of course, he stopped right in front of Shante for her to talk back to him. "You know, or you trying to find out how we do," she says jokingly as a challenge. He looked and gave a light smile, and she continued saying, "Nah but you were right about this party. We love it though." "If y'all need anything just signal for me but ask your two friends, can I turn them up one time." Shante looked at his shirt and got cautious. He seen her eyes squench and he asked her, "What's wrong," while looking down at his self? "Well first, we don't know your name. Second, we not trying to get kidnapped, and we don't know what turn them up means. Third, that shirt means that you are a Q-Dog. You didn't just have that on." "Are you scared of fraternity brothers are something?" "No, I'm not but I have seen y'all act parties and if I wasn't just as bad, I would be scared of y'all. Y'all to touchy touchy for most liking. Look though, definitely turn my homegirls up. I'm not gone tell'em. Just come grab'em." "Okay that's a bet," he says and walks off. Little did Shante know; the Qs were about to take the club over for the next fifteen minutes. The DJ played DMX Ruff

Ryder Anthem to signal the Qs to get to the floor. The security helps them get people off the floor. As members went and got women from the crowd. Linda and Eve were two out of the women picked. 'All you ladies pop yo pussy like this' The women in the club heard that intro from Khia and started rocking while Eve was being lifted over one of the guys shoulders with her pussy lined with his mouth. She is hollering and the women edging her on. The guy putting on a show as if he was eating her while squatting at the same time. He got finished performing for the ladies in the audience and passed her to the other guy. Linda was placed in a seat by the guy that chose her and she had her hands over her mouth watching Eve being lifted and tossed. The guy walked over to Linda and instructed for her to stand up and turn to the chair and touch it. Making her bend over with clear instructions to arch her back. She done it and looked at her home girls and they were piping her up to show out. The Q's circled her and started doing a dance and right on que, Trina verse to you don't know Nan was switched on and the women started rapping. Qs made the scene look as if she was really on the words of the verse. 'You don't know nan hoe, who been the places I been, who can spend the grands that I spend, fuck bout five or six best friends' The club was rocking and every woman in attendance were rapping to Trina verse. Every guy acted as if they had her making it seem like as if she really would fuck five or six best friends. They put on a good show like always for the women. The guy returned her to her section after they were through performing the club and everybody got back to partying. As the night wore down, they had had so much fun that they forgot to get drunk. Linda sold two of her bottles to a guy for three hundred a piece. They had a great time and of course was all on Live and all other social media platforms showing what a good time they were having. They start letting the club out and the girls decided to go to the Waffle House. It was 3:30am. Shante tells them to order they food to go because of the day party they are hosting tomorrow. She then calls the other girls that's trailing them to tell them,

"Is y'all food under my name like I told y'all to put it," says Shante as she pulls into the Waffle House that they googled." "Yes girl," they all responded to her. "Okay Imma be in and out." She parked and got out and immediately the parking lot eyes shifted to her. The dress she had on hugged her curves like a child that misses his mother and sees her again. Add to her ass cheeks rotating like two glazed hams on Thanksgiving. Finger licking good. Lime green Luxe dress that has a modern opulence. The zip closure was hidden, and it also has a thigh split to it. She was runway ready. Red lip stick, red earrings, red heels. Jerria looked in the Waffle House and she definitely know men were offering to pay for the meal. "I should have went in there myself because I know I could have saved me some money. I know Shante not about to except anything. Watch she don't bring us no change back because she didn't take them niggas money," says Jerria. As Shante said, she was in and out. The food was ready when she walked in. She gets in the car and hands the food to the two in her car and then gives the other car of girls they bag. They get to the house and Jerria says, "Girl now you know you could have saved all of us some coins by letting them niggas pay for this." "Girl you still on that," Shante reaches into her pocketbook and grabs a twenty-dollar bill and continues, "Girl here you go." "Why you acting like that? I'm just saying, use them niggas like atm machines, right?" "That had nothing to do with feeding yourself. Sometimes you have to show men that your womanhood is not up for debate, and you can take care of yourself. We using men as atm machines because we want them to be able to bring something to the table. Yes, it's still fuck'em and them same guys we might see again this week now knows they have to come harder. Dam girl, think long term approach. I can't teach you everything," she says to Jerria. They continued chatting and eating their food. When they were done, they headed to their rooms and went to sleep.

"Wake up homie," Ricky Jr calls Kim with excitement in his voice! "Boy it's too early for all that energy," she said while stretching and yawning. "Long night I see. It's 11:30am. Y'all still in bed on vacation. Y'all behind. I will be over in bout an hour." "We got in around 3:30am and went to sleep around 4:30 or 5am." "Well, you should be straight. That's over seven hours asleep so you should be balanced out." She yawns again and says, "Okay I'm bout to get up." "Aight. See you in a minute." They hang up. She gets up and takes a shower, brush her teeth, and determines her hairstyle and wardrobe. She puts on a bikini with a schoolgirl skirt to wear over her bottoms. She goes to the kitchen and put on a pot of Folgers. While putting the coffee on, she playfully sings, "The best part of waking up. Is Folgers in your cup." Hazelnut creamer and four spoons of sugar.

Rita came into the kitchen and playfully start sniffing in the air. She playfully touches the stove and looked in the microwave and said to Kim, "Nah you trying to take the easy way out. Fuck that coffee. You were the first one up so you basically agreed to cook breakfast for everyone." "Rita go to sleep and definitely start over. Cause you tried it. I got you some coffee over there. It will wake you up. That's my contribution to one of y'all fixing breakfast. See Imma even fix your cup for you," she says as she fixed Rita a cup. "Ain't nothing funny. And hand me the French vanilla," Rita says with a playful attitude. Rita got some food out of the refrigerator and said, "Since your lazy ass don't want to cater to us. Imma make all of us a ham and cheese omelet with this ham sandwich meat." "Girl that's fine with me. Is it me or are you sore also. Usually, a bitch will be hungover from dranking to much, but I feel like I worked out yesterday. My legs sore." "I bet you do the way you were getting lose. That dress didn't stop shit. You weren't bullshitting last night girl." They both start referencing songs they hadn't ever heard before from Quad City DJs, 12 Gauge, Freak Nasty, and a couple more artists. Also mimicking dances, they were doing last night. Ricky Jr walked right in the front door and said, "Y'all don't know what kinds of people around y'all. I should not be able to walk straight in here. It's some real creeps in this world." "Yea you actually right about that. I don't know how we slipped like that," Kim says as she walks to him to give him a hug. "Yea but Rita. You look like you might know a little something on that stove. How bout you make your boy one of them omelets." "What's in it for me? I look at that like I'm serving a nigga." "O My God! Wouldn't that be different for ya. Friendship is what's in it for ya, and its practice for when you get you a nigga because you definitely should know how to serve your man. That's not a bad thing no matter what y'all lil divas think." "Yea you would say that. My name is Rita. And I'm the prize so I'm the one that should be served." "Your man definitely should serve you also but it's a two-way street," he says while shaking his head at her response and feel of entitlement. He continued, "But home girl, don't let that come between me and an omelet this morning. Fuck with the kid. I mean I am bout to turn y'all up a notch. I'm bout to bring the stuff in now for the party." Kim followed him out the door to the car. Brand new All Black Range Rover Autobiography with Forgiato black 22's on it. "I see ya," Kim says alluding to his SUV. "O this light kinfolk." "Well, shid it looks like something I can't afford." "Me and Bruh gone get you there. Don't worry. Just be patient." He popped the hatch to the back and opened the doors to the sexy black SUV. "You must already had this planned in your head with all this shit." "Well kind of sorta did, but it's better to do it at this big as house anyway. Makes it more intimate instead of a building." He had 300 chocolate covered strawberries, 500 candy grapes, 100 bottles combined of wine, champagne, and liquor. Glasses, finger foods, and plates. The grapes and strawberries were made by Candy Man of Chattanooga. They get everything carried in and put the chocolate strawberries along with the candy grapes in the refrigerator. By this time everyone had woken up and come downstairs. Rita fixed everyone an omelet and handed it to them as they came in. "Jr did your cousin come down with you this weekend," Shante asks with sneaky eyes. "Nah. He is in Chattanooga doing a basketball camp at Howard High School. He had forgot about this weekend when he planned the camp so he not going to make it down here." Shante and Kim make eye contact on a bitch you ain't slick vibe playfully. Jerria was showing clear signs of having an attitude towards Jr, but he wasn't paying it any attention as everyone carried on in conversation.

The party got started and everyone was actually ready to party. Due to vacation, people were actually on time unlike night parties. Jr's guest of the men he was referring to get their around three though. The scene was single adults that were lawyers, sports agents, high end car salesmen and real estate developers, professional athletes, and pharmaceuticals. Jr introduced Linda to the real estate invites, and

they engaged in conversation deeply right off.
She took a liking to a guy by the name of
Quentin Jennings. Light skin, clean cut, 6'3,
220lbs, athletic frame with penitentiary arms.
Linda graced the men eyes with an all-white
bikini from Louis Vuitton. Legs immaculately
waxed with an also perfect panty line. A white
cowgirl hat for the sun and her hair slayed up
under the hat. When she walked, her ass gave
stripped vibes with the jiggles of softness.
Quentin slowly kept grabbing her attention by
catering to her knowledge of being an agent. He
was a broker, investor, and developer. He was
serving of what she is chasing in which made
him sort of a fantasy guy in the flesh for her.
After both of them secluded themselves and

drank three bottles of wine amongst each other they started feeling the liquid. Linda felt herself about to catch a body count. "Whaaaat. Let me go jump in this water. Get this body wet under this Miami sun," she says seductively to him, and he caught it. "O baby I promise you. Getting you wet want be a problem that I need a pool for. Just tell me that's what you want, and I can make that happen naturally," he responds back with confidence. She looked back over her shoulders flirtatiously and added an extra pep to her step as he watched her walk to the pool. She walked in and sat on the steps. Everybody was mingling and feeling each other out. Jr was doing a good job at hosting and entertaining. He had brung is personal patna DJ Hollywood

Oompa down to Miami with him and he provided music for the party. New connections were made and possible flings for the weekend. Seven thirty hit and all the guests had left except for Jr and DJ Oompa. "A y'all. We brung our clothes and shit for tonight. Do y'all mind if we shower and just leave from here," Jr asked the girls? Eve plops down on the couch and says, "Boy don't nobody care, but that party was a well mixture of the right people. You want to be able to control the crowd like that all the time, but you definitely should look into hosting. Us professional people love to kick back also. Maybe members only club." "Well, this the first time I ever done it and you right it went good. I might look into it. Is Chattanooga ready for a members only club. Shit sounds freaky though," they all laugh after he said it. "They are upgrading Chattanooga and like I said, a members only spot might actually be okay." "I might look into it, but basketball keeps me busy. I got to get me one of these 300 million contracts, so I got to work on my game around the clock. Unless you offering to run it," he asked looking at her with what's up eyes. "If it makes sense money wise and it don't interfere with what I got going on then I probably be in. Let's talk about it when we get back and before you leave the city." "Bet." "But I will say though. I might need to get into some form of entertainment. I thought my little thirty-three dollars an hour was good until I was talking to these people. I would have never thought a car salesman made that kind of money. I bet I won't judge any jobs by title anymore. Everything depends on the position and how much work you willing to put into your craft I see." "Aww shit. Look at Rita sounding all sympathetic and educated on something more than her own thoughts," Jr says folding his arms as a sign of being impressed." "Boy boo. I got good sense, but they did open my eyes to some things. I see that they only talked in percentages, group economics, and monopolizing the businesses they are a part of no matter what the business is. The last thing I noticed is that not one of them had one form of income. The minimum was three for everyone I talked to but the ones that were at seven figures had at least six things making revenue. I was like a kid in school with no ADHD. They had my full attention." "Nah u was a damsel in need of saving or might I say a hot little woman ready to jump on something," Jerria says playing. "Girl probably all the above, but they had my full attention though. Jerria again responded and said, "Well shout out to them, but my second job is tricking niggas and I ain't ashamed of it." Without looking at Jerria, Jr responded and said, "Did you trick them? Or did they score?" "Excuse me," she says while rolling her eyes and tries scowl him with words on how niggas ain't shit but dogs and this and that. "Man, you just did all that and didn't answer my question.

Did you trick them, or did they score?" "How I look at it is I tricked them? Ain't nobody getting anything from me without taking care of me. They want one thing so I will see to it that I'm well compensated." "So, if you know they only want one thing. And they achieved it, so how did you trick them. O you got a gift in the process in which he was happy to give. Now with that, I can say you got an even transaction but nah. I can't say that's an even trade because a woman's body is a temple. You are devaluing it. But keep on tricking these niggas," he shakes his head and continues, "Have a little bit more care about who enters your soul. But it's not considered your soul. How could it be that or anything you hold at high regard if you basically look at it as a means to make some money.?" "You didn't seem to have a problem with my terms when I presented them to you," she says thinking she was about to shut him up. He laughed and said, "Baby girl. I just said all that. And your come back is that I basically paid you for some pussy. Did you not hear that the worth is what you put on it and any man will be willing to pay for it. You have to view it as a temple before I do. The problem with men is we try to approach women who don't view it as a temple, so you are right actually. If I liked you, I should not have been willing to play them type games. But hey, it was fun. When I get some more money, I will hit you up," he said with the most sarcastic voice in human history while looking at the keys of his Range Rover. The girls actually wanted to help their friend but couldn't deny the things he was saying. Reality is dangerous when thrown in your face. Kim gulped her last shot of wine as a sense of dam he told her. Jerria rolled her eyes and walked off. Shante shook her head with a smile and Rita was texting a guy she met at the party. It seems like everyone was stuck for words. Jr smiled at her rolling her eyes and continued while clapping his hands once, "My bad y'all but that needed to be said and Kim you better not be on what she on or I'm telling unk on you." "Boy I don't have nothing to do with that." "Yea aight. To get back on vacation time. Look. I got a booth at Club M2 tonight. My patnas said they're not going out. They just gone walk the strip for some odd reason. I got it because Slatt Zy and BaggLyfe Tip are performing from Chattanooga show I had to show the home team some love. It's enough room for y'all if y'all wants to join me. I think only three of us are still going. Me, Oompa, and Quentin." "O hell yea. We with that. Let me take a cat nap and I will be ready to rock and roll again," says Linda. "Well then. That's settled. Y'all might as well follow me down there. Imma leave here at 10:30pm. I have to be there before 11:30pm or they will resale the section. They ain't bullshitting down here." Everyone lounged around the house feeling the aftereffects from the day party. Time passed by, and it was around nine. Everyone had started getting ready to go out. Jr came down styling and profiling. Brown Burberry shorts, white button down collared imprinted Burberry shirt with the belt. Burberry shoes that matched the full pattern on the shirt. Presidential Rolex watch and two iced out necklaces. Shirt unbuttoned to show his ice and toned chest. Oompa went with an all-Versace outfit with a gold Medusa head in the middle of the shirt. All the women came out of their rooms and complimented both of them. All the women smelling good and looking very edible. "Oh, I'm bout to be y'all number one hater tonight. Every dude that ask about y'all or come up to y'all Imma throw my arms around you and introduce myself as your man." "Well, you can do it for me if they don't look like they are up to par," says Linda. "All I'm saying is dam Rick, you could have been brung me around these beautiful women. Y'all are looking very beautiful tonight, but let me formally introduce myself properly to you," he says and extended his hand out to Eve. "How are you? Imma DJ that goes by Oompa, but I would like for you to call me David." "David. I'm Eve. It's nice to meet you and you look very handsome tonight." "I would like to get to know you after this vacation. Don't want you to think I'm just trying to get a vacation girlfriend so after we leave Miami, I would like to take you out once we get back." "Well, how you know I don't want a vacation boyfriend though. Don't sell yourself short trying to impress me. Although I do appreciate the gesture," she says with a seductress smile. Everyone eyes were on them, and the women admired his boldness to come at Eve in front of all of them. "Well, if that's what you want, I would like to provide that also, but I definitely would like to continue that into normal activities of us. I don't want to just be your vacation fling." "Hmmm. I might be a little impressed because most men are excited about being a fling. Let me tell you this though before you sample this," she says and sexually moves close to him. She bit her bottom lip, squinched her eyes, and lifted her head to him as in submission and continued saying, "This pussy will fuck your life up. I will quit my job and just spend your money." "Well with all due respect to your good pussy. But you see I know what kind of dick and mouth I would be giving you. And that along will motivate you to keep your job because you will love the fact of accomplishing things in life because I would be your number one motivator. Just as you wouldn't talk to a man that couldn't do anything for you. I wouldn't talk to a woman that couldn't do anything for me, so quitting your job isn't an option." "Well excuse me daddy," she says flirtatiously. Jerria turned her lips sideways at his words and said, "Man. Girl fuck what these niggas talking bout. Let's ride. Y'all can finish that convo at the club." "I actually agree with that," Jr says as everyone moved towards the door. They dealt with the same parking war as the night before and paid nicely to park close to the club. Oompa covered their charge though. As they walked up, Quentin was already up there securing the table. "Perfect timing," Quentin says as he was about to get escorted by security to the booth. Jr and the crew joined him. Quentin saw Linda and stuck his arm out like an escort down the walkway of a wedding. She took his arm, and they walked in together. As they got to their booth, Slatt and Bagglyfe were already in their VIP booths having a Miami nightlife time. Bottles coming along with the attention of who they are. All of em greeted each other with love. The other three floor booths were also people from Chattanooga that were supporting their hometown. Also, artist Frank White, J-Mac, BO, each had their own booth. Each person had their separate entourage, but they all were there as one. When Slatt went on, they all hit the floor and let it be known that Chattanooga was in Miami this weekend. Quentin had Linda full attention despite every male that was in attendance. Slatt started performing Gangsta Prodigy and Linda showed Quentin that her mother gave her something soft in her rear as he grinded on her. Brown on brown Armani Exchange slacks and Polo. The Aramani Polo emblem was on the shirt in red lettering. He sported red Gucci shoes, red Gucci belt, with his shirt tucked in to show the belt. Bust down

Cartier watch that caught every light in the club. She grinded harder against him trying to feel his package. He knew her senses would automatically wonder what he would feel like inside of her. Everyone had a great time and put on for the city. Club started closing at 3am and they all walked out together then went their separate ways to their cars. Quentin stopped to talk to Linda. "So, what are you doing Sunday Ms. Linda?" "I guess party some more. It's Miami," she said in an excited voice. "Well look. On Sunday you are going to the game with me. It's game seven of the Eastern Conference Finals. Do you watch sports?" "Of course. That would be unamerican not to." "Aww shit. Where have you been all my life? I will pick you up around seven." "Okay." He gave her a firm hug and she felt secure in his arms. He opened the door for her and looked in the SUV and said, "Drive safe ladies." Linda was smiling so hard because she knew her girls were about to grill her for being wide open. "Girl if you don't close your mouth and put them icy whites up. You feeling that man ain't cha," Shante asked? "Girl. In my mind he done fucked me twice and gave me chills." "Dam his conversation that good?" "Then it's throwing me off because he hasn't really attempted to fuck me. I'm not used to that. This muthafucker to in control and a bitch like it." They all burst out laughing. Linda continues, "And by the way. I won't be with y'all Sunday because he is taking me to the Miami

Heat game," she said in a playful boastful voice. Kim breathed in heavily and said, "O hell nah. Jr claimed that it was sold out. I'm jealous but happy he is showing you a good time friend." They all continue talking and playing with Linda. Shante phone vibrated and it's a text from Brandon. It reads, "Your ass bet not be paying any of them niggas no attention or I know something. Have fun but don't get hurt." She sent back a GIF of Beyonce rolling her eyes and popping gum.

Monday comes and the girls were at the airport ever so exhausted. "Someone didn't come home last night," says Eve. "Right. Gone try to sneak in at seven this morning. You not slick. Give us the story while we wait on this flight," says Rita. "Well. We went to the game and that's about it." "Stop fucking playing girl," says Rita laughing. "Okay Okay! As y'all know, he picked me up for the game. He was a guest in one of his colleagues suite and that's how he was able to bring me." "Ewwwww Colleague. Such professional words," Rita playfully says. "We watched the game and I listened and watched him talk business with the people there. After the game, he took me to a spa. Ion know how he pulled that off that late. He told them to massage my entire body for thirty minutes. Two women were on me and lord it felt so good that I almost had a gay moment. One massaged my scalp, temples, and shoulders. The other massaged these ass cheeks and calves. The whole time I'm wondering why my pussy soooooo wet. The lady literally stepped out the room and let me wipe off, but I was confused because I wasn't horny. They come back in and finish my top side. My thighs, chins, breast, and neck. I was defenseless. He comes in and he shakes their hand. I was about to get up and he says no stay relaxed. He pulls some grapes from a bag he was holding and hands them to me. He slowly talks to me about how beautiful I am. How much he loved my company. How he needs me in his life. Then he started massaging my feet. At that moment, it was like he moved every negative vibe in me out of my life. Every time he firmly pressed the balls of my feet; it was like it sent an electric shock to my clit. I closed my eyes and fed myself grapes. All of a sudden, he had worked his mouth to my clit," she closed her eyes and shook her head. Placing her hands on her thighs she looked at them and said, "Girl. He ate my pussy so good that I ascended out of my body and watched him in disbelief that someone tongue could make me feel like that. He gave me the orgasm of my dreams. He thoroughly wiped me off. We left and went back to his suite at the Fountain Blue. I was on cloud ten waiting for some dick. We got inside. He removed my clothes slowly while looking in my eyes. He removed my clothes slowly while never breaking eye contact. His body looked so dam good to me when he stood back and took off his clothes. Everything firm and smooth. Not bushy, shaved, but not bald. Lord, I hate a nigga that's bald. I would get a bitch if I didn't want to feel any hair. He was everything and didn't even know it. Instead of just putting his dick in me. This slick muthafucker spooned me holding me like treasure that has gold locked in it and whispered in my ear that I am safe as long as I'm in his arms. That I can relax. That he will make sure that I am protected from harm. Then he told me I am the woman he needs." "Dam Girl. You for real," everyone asked while blushing. "Bitch hell nah. That's my fantasy date." They all fall out laughing. "Girl, you got me over here all happy for your day and shit and telling us a fantasy of yours, but bitch that would be idea," Kim says. "But for real. We went to Catch of the Day seafood restaurant then to the game. We didn't do all that shit I said but I did have a good time with him." "Well, that's a good sign. Follow it. Give that man a chance," says Eve. Little did they know, the story was real, but she seen their faces and decided not to keep that in their mind. Females are dangerous with that type of information.

It's June 6th and everyone's back to their normal life. Eve has a spark from the day party in Miami though. She texts Jr and says, "Jr. This is Eve. Can I take you to dinner Thursday on my off day?" He responds, "Am I reading this right. You're taking me? How high is your fever? Is your blood pressure up? Is this really Eve," firm and smooth. Not bushy, shaved, but not bald. Lord, I hate a nigga that's bald. I would get a bitch if I didn't want to feel any hair. He was everything and didn't even know it. Instead of just putting his dick in me. This slick muthafucker spooned me holding me like treasure that has gold locked in it and whispered in my ear that I am safe as long as I'm in his arms. That I can relax. That he will make sure that I am protected from harm. Then he told me I am the woman he needs." "Dam Girl. You for real," everyone asked while blushing. "Bitch hell nah. That's my fantasy date." They all fall out laughing. "Girl, you got me over here all happy for your day and shit and telling us a fantasy of yours, but bitch that would be idea," Kim says. "But for real. We went to Catch of the Day seafood restaurant then to the game. We didn't do all that shit I said but I did have a good time with him." "Well, that's a good sign. Follow it. Give that man a chance," says Eve. Little did they know, the story was real, but she seen their faces and decided not to keep that in their mind. Females are dangerous with that type of information.

It's June 6th and everyone's back to their normal life. Eve has a spark from the day party in Miami though. She texts Jr and says, "Jr. This is Eve. Can I take you to dinner Thursday on my off day?" He responds, "Am I reading this right. You're taking me? How high is your fever? Is your blood pressure up? Is this really Eve," ending with a couple laughing emojis. "You got jokes. Meet me at J. Alexanders at eight." "Aight. Thursday it is." It's four o'clock pm and Eve, Rita, and Kim are on their last lunch break in the breakroom together. "Girls. Are we wasting time working for others or are we doing what we have to do to survive in this world?" "Well Eve, I would say thirty dollars an hour is not surviving. That's doing great, but I would say yes, we are just doing what we have to do to survive. Nothing wrong with that," says Rita. "So, we basically go to school for, well I went to K-12, four years at Austin Peay and for one year of Chattanooga State Nursing Program which is a total of eighteen fucking years to make approximately seventy-one thousand with overtime a year." Kim takes a bite of her sandwich and ask, "Shid what's wrong with seventy-one thousand?" "Absolutely nothing. Salute to everyone in the world that is making that because it's a nice living. On the flipside, at Jr Day party at our spot in Miami I met a guy with a GED that makes one-hundred thousand off selling cars. Started out at a small dealership by the name of Wright's and worked his way up. He moved to LA and landed a job at a high-end dealership. Even the Quentin guy had no education. He also had a GED. After that he took a two-week real estate course to be an agent then followed that three years later with a broker course. Now he is an investor and developer. By the looks of him and his demeanor, he at least at seven figures. All I am saying is there is more than just clocking in, but you got to jump out there." "Eve what are you getting at," asked Kim? "Let's all three of us start our own Assistant Living on the medical housing business." "Nah. I'm too scared of the what ifs. What if we don't get any patients? What if? What if? What if," Rita repeats the question? "I'm just not a risk taker, but I will promise you this. If you start it, I will work for you and bust my ass for you like I have done this slave plantation of a company," Kim says. "I'm going to hold you to that Kim," Eve says giving her a high five. Rita gets a text from Joshua. "Hi! Rita I'm sorry if I offended you, but now I have a business proposition for you. My wife needs assistance while I'm at work. I understand you already have a job, but we can give forty-five an hour. When I go out of town, we can pay fifty an hour because those days will be 24hrs needed. She's my life," he says through text. "Bitch. You right here speaking on business and my shaky ass just got asked a business question. I'm still scared, so I'm going to refer you." "What's going on," Eve asked? "Joshua just offered me a job for forty-five dollars an hour while he works and fifty dollars an hour for when he travels to watch his wife because I will need to spend the whole day with her." "Well got damn. Look at God. I'm gone ask y'all again. Do y'all want to jump out on faith with me," Eve says looking like a kid on

Christmas. "Nah, I'm sure. I'm happily about to get you your first patient though." "Cool girl. Tell him the agency name is," a short pause gauzing in air as she thinks and then responds and says, "Hell I don't know yet. Just tell him my name and background. I'm clocking back in for the last hour and a half, but I'm putting my two week's notice in tomorrow. Bye y'all and thank you Rita," says Eve as she walks off. While she walked off, Rita texted Joshua. "Joshua, I hope I find a partner at life as you have. I must turn the position down, but I'm doing so to put your wife in great professional hands. The girl's name Eve that was with me the night I met with you at the pool hall has started her own sitting care business. She has many accolades as a Registered Nurse. She will and can do it the job the best anyone else can. I will stay your friend when you need to talk." As he received the text he responded and said, "Okay Thank you. Our kids are here until Sunday. I need her to start next Monday, but she needs to come on that Sunday to get a tour. They're only giving her a year to live. Fucking doctors." Rita reads and feels sorry for him but is impressed with the love he has for his woman. She texted back Eve cell phone number. Then she clocked in also.

Dontae had an after meeting with Brewer Chevrolet dealership. Dontae wasn't worried about getting a building to start off with. He wanted his contracts to purchase him a building. The owner of the dealership name is Josh. He and Dontae grew up playing sports with each other. Josh had worked at a dealership for fifteen years before securing his own car dealership. Ricky and Brandon had let Josh know that Dontae had started his detail company, so it was a no brainer to give his friend the contract. The next day after the meeting Dontae went back to the dealership along with Ricky, Brandon, and his nephew in which is Dontae business partner. They walk in and gets greeted. "Dontae," Josh says yelling in a happy to see you tone. He walks to greet him with a man embrace. "What's good bossman? I want to say before we get started that I appreciate the meeting and that I am proud you set a goal and accomplished it." "A I appreciate you saying that. It ain't because I gave you the contract is it," Josh responds, and both start laughing. He continues and says, "I'm just fucking witcha. My office is right there in the corner. Y'all go wait for me in there. I got to make sure I close on this sell right quick. Give me fifteen minutes." "Take your time. We are going to help ourselves to some water and popcorn." "Go ahead," Josh says as he walks off to wrap up the sale. He approached two men with a MCM duffle bag. They were twin brothers named Lloyd and Terry. They had come to spend cash, so their importance was top priority at the moment. "Awww fellas. Look. Are y'all sure y'all can handle these bad boys. I mean I have got cars with smaller engines if you want. Ion want nothing to be too much power for ya now. And those cars are cheaper also," Josh says knowing how to make a man ego say fuck it. They both looked at him like their nuts had dropped. Lloyd responded and said, "Man. Are both of these fully loaded. Matter of fact, which two are the most expensive." Josh walks them in front of the two Corvette Zr1's. One blue and the other black. The blue one is convertible. "This convertible is 135k and the hard top is 131k. Both have only been on my lot for 4 days. No one has even come to test drive em so you both would be the first to put horsepower to the engines in them. Also, they the fastest on the lot and edges the hellcat by a small margin." "Well let's walk into the building and handle things then." When they walked through doors of the building, they both through bags at Josh feet and Tery says, "Aight look we gone drive them off today. The money in the bags. We will come back tomorrow and sign all the papers. Is that a problem." Josh bent down to unzip both bags to make sure money was in both and smiled. He stood up with both bags now on his shoulders and says, "Nah that's cool. Let me get the keys for y'all. Perfect choices also. Don't be out there showing out and wreck before you sign everything tomorrow," Josh says as he walks to his office to throw the bags in there and grab the keys. "A we gotcha. And we want our change too nigga. Just leave it in the bags with the title for when we come back tomorrow," Lloyd says. "Cool. Come back tomorrow at two and everything will be ready. All you will have to do is sign things and that's it." Both nod their heads in response. He gives them the keys and they pull off burning rubber. Josh gets back to his office. He walks through his office door and says, "Well Dontae. You know you, my man. 100 grand, but Imma go with this white boy. He just what I need, and I can fire him with no remorse if he fucks up. I don't want nothing messing up our history." Dontae and his nephew looked at each other. Dontae was defeated but kept it professional for his nephew as to stay a positive example. Dontae extends his hand to Josh and says, "You are still my homeboy and I'm still proud of you starting your own dealership my boy. Keep me in mind for the future and pass my number alone to others that might be looking for service." "Man, I thought we were about to get into an argument. You messed it up for me," Josh says shortly laughing then says, "But nah. Imma give you the contract. I got a contract for you to sign. It basically states that I am hiring your company to detail all cars here at forty-five hundred a month. You use your own supplies, but of course I will provide the water. Matter of fact, you do have driver license and insurance right." "Yea." "Good. I ask because if you didn't, you wouldn't be able to move the cars." "Cool. I

accept, but I'm a new company trying to have sturdy legs. I was hoping to also secure this contract for two years and hopefully you will keep renewing the business. I promise to do my part even better because of our history. I won't slack off because of our history feeling like I'm entitled because we grew up together. I'm going to work hard just as I would for a stranger."
"Well, I hope so. I might be able to take you in the door at other car lots in the city. If I did though, would I make commission on the contract. Let's say, ten percent on any contract I bring to the table that you sign off on." "I wouldn't have a problem with that. Nah I wouldn't have a problem with that at all." "Cool. Give me two months and I should have some

things lining up. A couple of dealerships are moving towards this. Upon referral and hiring though, you better not embarrass me nor yourself." "I hear you loud and clear." They shake hands. Josh also shakes Dontae nephew hand and gives them the pen to sign the papers. He directs them to the dotted lines of the papers, and they finalize everything right at that moment. Dontae texted Kim and told her the good news. He and his nephew talk for a minute going over what this means for the company and how they gone separate funds for this and that. His nephew was equally excited as his uncle although he didn't fully understand everything, but he knew it was good to add guaranteed money to the business.

Everyone always knows that more money is good. Dontae went to Facebook and posted pictures of the deal going through while sending a positive message to people trying to go in business and spoke highly of his nephew accepting guidance.

Thursday June 9th came, and Shante got off at three. She and Brandon had the house to themselves for at least two hours. "I told you the next *splack* time you gave me this *splack* pussy *splack splack* I was going to give you this dick," he says as he is talking to her while he pounds her in the missionary position. He got her legs spread like a woman giving birth with her knees bent up into her chest. "Ewwww shit boy. That's my fucking spot," she hollers in between falsetto moans. He keeps his steady pounding pace driving her body to bliss. He looked her in her eyes and was getting turned on from the now starting of her rolling her eyes and pussy getting wetter. "Is that pussy bout to come." "Yes baby. Fuck. O my God." "Not God. This Brandon hitting this pussy. Say the right fucking name," he says as he started hitting it even faster and harder. *Splack splack splack splack splack splack splack splack* She squeezed her eyes and dug her nails in his back and enjoyed her orgasm flowing out of her. Her body convulsed under him. "That pussy feel better now," he said in her ear in a baritone voice. He stopped moving. He was letting his nut go back down distracting her with sexual conversation. "Shut up. Baby its very wet down there." "Nah that's sloppy." "Well, it's getting cold." "O so you through," he says kissing her gently on her neck letting her legs down. "I thought you were." He closed her legs almost all the way and put his legs right on the side of hers making his dick be as one with her clit. "Dam that dick hard baby." "You the only one it gets this way for." She hunched upwards strongly repeatedly clinching her pussy lips every time she comes back down. When she hunched up, he moved forward making him get a little deeper each time and cause traction on her clit. Her clit started getting very stimulated again. After repeating the motion and him placing her right titty in his mouth. Suckling her nipple as if it was a clit itself gave her even more heightened stimulation. "Damn boy. I'm about to cum again." "Cum then. Who is stopping you? Keep that same pace though and feel that in your soul. Don't rush it." "Yes daddy. Tell me how you want this pussy. That turns me on." His grunts got a little louder and it turned her on because she knew he was about to cum with her. She locked her legs holding him in place. As they began to climax together, their lips found each other kissing each other deeply as both of they bodies became as one and released as one. They gave each other soul snatching gazing eye contact while each of them pleased each other into exhaustion. He rolled off her in heavy breathing. He kept contact with her by laying his hand on her stomach. "I can get use to that," she says turning on her side facing him. "Me too baby. Me too." "So, what's up? How are we playing this? I'm asking because I'm already going against shit. Men are approaching from every direction and I'm turning them down. I haven't accepted any money nor gifts from anyone out of pure respect for you," she leans up and says and continues, "And before it creeps in your head, know I didn't fuck people for money. I tricked men out of money. Give them a fantasy of one day they might fuck, and they come off of everything. By the time they realize I'm not fucking them I done been done got everything I probably want. I want to fuck you. It's a very big difference." "I appreciate you addressing that before I could even ask. And I'm just having fun as you are at this current moment and lord am I glad you chose me to want to fuck because that pussy good." She hits him playfully in the stomach. "Ought. But look. Let's go on a couple dates and see where we stand before I leave back out. Is that fair to say. It's easy for me to make you mine from great sex but let's make sure we are worth each other's time." "I agree with that. Just be honest with me is all I ask but let me get up before one of these bitches pull up." She gives him a kiss and gets out of bed. Jr calls Brandon as soon as she gets out of bed. He answers on the third ring. "What up kinfolk?" "Shit just having a hard time with this decision." "What you got going on lil bruh," Brandon asked in a concerned big brother voice? "Bruh I'm bout to go on a date with Eve." "Shid what's wrong with that?" "Nothing. And she is paying for it so absolutely nothing." "Well then I am lost." "I'm trying to figure out do I tell her about me fucking Jerria or not." "Fam that's to close. You got to tell her. Hell, they so close, Eve probably already knows actually." "Yea you right about that. I'm thinking too hard about all this from my guilty conscious. Eve probably seriously just wants to have dinner and talk business. I'm saying though G, what if we end up fucking. I'm letting you know now bruh. I'm not turning down no pussy from Eve. That would be unamerican." They both burst out laughing and Jr continue, "but I don't want to be a nigga she feel trying to run through a click. Unfortunate things just happen sometimes." "Well, how hard you thinking, I think you should tell her if the conversation starts going towards you two going on dates and things. If she doesn't know she probably be mad if she trying to talk to you on that level, but women crazy beings G. She gone be mad, but it won't be a deal breaker because you the one that told her. It wasn't rubbed in her face. Now you gone be confused because she still might have an attitude but for some reason, she gone still fuck with you. Women confusing like that. Now, you will be a fuck nigga if you tell her after you get the pussy."

"So, tell her on don't tell her?" A short pause comes about, and Brandon says, "If you care how she feels, then tell her. If you just trying up the score, then don't tell her, but losing respect of a woman is not worth getting a score up."

"Dam you right about that. Aight Bruh. Imma hit cha later on."

Eve pulls up to J. Alexanders at seven thirty pm so she can have her paperwork in order and her pitch to Jr about going into business or giving her the loan to further her business. She grabs her phone to text him. "I'm here already. I'm telling you so you won't be on black people time." He replied back, "Okay. I'm hitting the interstate downtown. Be there shortly." Eve cautiously didn't dress up because she didn't want him to walk in and feel any sexual tension. She wore her nursing scrub, but even with that on she was a curvaceous woman. It fitted her body, so although she wasn't trying, he walked in and still got an even better view of her body measurements, and the scrub made her ass cheeks loosely move when she walked. He caught view of all of her when she went to the ladies' room. "Got dam Eve. How didn't I notice all that before? Mercy," he said to himself. She comes back to the table and as she walks from behind him, she playfully taps him on his shoulder. He playfully acts like she was too strong and that the tap hurt him, "Ought," he grabbed his shoulder playing and continues, "What I do already?"

"Being a man. I seen you watching my ass while I was walking to the restroom." "Lie. How you see me and didn't even turn around to look?" "Boy its mirrors in here." "Nah you just know because you know you working with something and to be real, I would say something wrong with me if I didn't look at it." "Yea Yea Yea Yea. Why do you look so tense? Relax dude." "Man let me be real from the start then. I hope you respect me keeping it real but it's what got me tensed. Um. Jerria and I did something once," he said it in a tone of regret. "Boy Boo. I don't care. I'm on something else. I told you that you sparked something in me introducing me to people that are taking risk on themselves." "Aww man I thought I had a chance." She cutely laughed and said, "See. Now, you look hard and want me. Jr when you want a woman, we can talk about that. Right now, I'm here on strictly business." Waitress walks up and ask, "May I take y'all order?" "Yes, um both of us will have the salmon dinner with fully loaded mashed potatoes and a sprite." "Are you good with that mister," the waitress says very flirtatious. Eve caught it and smiled like a friend. "Um actually know. Instead of the sprite I will take a water, but she is paying so everything else is good with me." "Yea water is better for your back and everything else. Do you still play?" Eve and Jr looked at each other and Jr was stuck like a baby caught by his mama, but he didn't understand why. Eve seen his expression and chuckled again because she thought it was cute the way he trying to be nice to the waitress but also not disrespect Eve. "Umm yea. I was overseas for 2yrs and just got picked up this year by the Magic. Been with them 2yrs. You follow the game." "Not really. I went to Notre Dame high school, but I vividly remember following your games in high school," she turned to Eve and said, "No disrespect to you." "O baby you crossed the if he was my man disrespect threshold moments ago. But he not mine so I can't be mad." The waitress eyes filled with joy, and she said, "So you're single," she asked with a flirtatious stance? Eve looking at her like the nerve of this bitch. Jr caught like a deer in headlights responds and says, "Ummm no disrespect to you but can we get our orders put in and that conversation is kind of inappropriate at this time don't you think. But like I said, it's no disrespect." "Non taking. I'm just finally happy I spoke to you. I will get this in right now." The waitress walks off and turns the order in. She immediately brings their drinks back and walks off. Eve watched his eyes to see if he would watch her and he passed that test because he didn't give her any attention. That impressed Eve. "Well before your fan club interrupted us, like I was telling you, I have a business proposal." "Aight talk to me. What do you have?" "I want to eventually open my own care center that caters to the elderly. Within the facility there would be several accommodating wings to also offer skilled long-term care, and health/hospitality and care. I got one patient that I'm about to start as assistant care, but I want to do a little more. This will keep my bills paid until I work towards getting what I just explained to you off the ground. I already basically quit my job so I'm about to go into full grind mode." "You already in this field though. What would you need from me?" "You can invest in me and be the CFO of the company. The medical field is a billion-dollar industry. Might even be a trillion-dollar industry and I'm just trying to get my percentage out of it." "So would you run things by me, or would you just let me know how much things cost, and I suppose to just jump at what you want. Will I have a say in the budget?" "Of course, you will. You are the Chief Financial Officer. That's in your description. I would just ask for a loan, but I feel you can already be looking at the retirement years. You young once but old forever." "Well, you right about that. How far along are you? Meaning do you have anything to show me what the startup cost will be for the facility?" "Well Linda gave me this printout of buildings that I can turn into a facility," she says while handing him the sheet with listings on it. She continues, "If you want, you can go with me to view the properties and hear everything or would you prefer me to do all the groundwork and let you know from there." "Man, I don't know nothing about this stuff.

What made you want to ask me to go in with you on this." "To be real, I just know you got the money, and you might as well invest it into someone you know. Keywords invest. I'm not asking for a handout, but it's easier for me to ask you than a bank because I would need to already make a certain amount and credit score has to be a certain amount. It's also something that will start building your portfolio at a young age." "Well since you put it like that, you can count me in," he points at one of the buildings and shows her the one he is pointing at and continues, "This one right here is the one we are getting. It's the biggest one so it means we have more room to do whatever it is you want to do. Plus, Highland Park is prime real estate. I think one point five is straight. Tell Linda to put in an offer for one point two million cash and let's see the response." "Okay I'm bout to get my state certifications and everything." The food comes and the waitress is smiling from ear to ear. "Y'all enjoy y'all food. It's hot like a home cooked meal for y'all," she says while leaving them two pitchers for they refill. One of water and one of sprite. They continue to conversate about different things that they both are interested in. They both were serving as motivators for each other at the moment which was refreshing to hear someone say just do that shit. "Well, lil Eve you not just a girl with a body and pretty face. You actually got something in that big head of yours." "Nigga don't talk about my head. I'm sensitive about that." "O my bad big head. I meant lil head. I meant beautiful," he says playfully. "You better quit playing and watch your mouth Lil Ricky, I meant lil dude, I meant Jr," she responds back playfully. "You got jokes with the lil dude comment." "Do I?" They looked in each other eyes, smiling and realized it turned into a flirting conversation and the silence was broken by Jr saying, "Girl let's get back to the house cause ain't nobody about to be playing with you. But I appreciate you giving me this opportunity." The waitress walks up with the bill and says, "Here go y'all bill. Take y'all time." "No! Here you go," Eve says. She takes the payment to her register and comes back with the receipt. "Here you go," the waitress says placing the receipt booklet on the table. "Let me see what I owe you," Jr says while grabbing the booklet. He opened the booklet and laughed. "What's funny?" "She wrote her number down." "This bitch bold. Let me see," Eve says grabbing the receipt book. She took her card out of the card holder latch and says, "Well I see she also gave you your food free, so I saved on that. I guess I think you for that." Jr. contemplating do he pose to ask for the number on the paper, but she quickly shut that down by saying, "And I don't worry about this number. Yea we here for business but you not about to getting bitches number in my presence. Ole girl bold though." They get up and walk outside in conversation. They had had such a good conversation that they weren't ready for it to end in such a short time. They decide to officially celebrate by staying in each other's company. They decided on the pool hall off Shallowford road. Jr texted Brandon and had told him to meet him and Eve at the pool hall off Shallowford. Brandon replied that he was on his way.

Made in the USA
Middletown, DE
17 August 2024